Date Due

A He

Books by Louise A. Vernon

Title	Subject
The Beggars' Bible	John Wycliffe
The Bible Smuggler	William Tyndale
Doctor in Rags	Paracelsus and Hutterites
A Heart Strangely Warmed	John Wesley
Ink on His Fingers	Johann Gutenberg
Key to the Prison	George Fox and Quakers
The King's Book	King James Version, Bible
The Man Who Laid the Egg	Erasmus
Night Preacher	Menno Simons
Peter and the Pilgrims	English Separatists, Pilgrims
The Secret Church	Anabaptists
Strangers in the Land	Huguenots
Thunderstorm in Church	Martin Luther

A Heart Strangely Warmed

Louise A. Vernon
Illustrated by Allan Eitzen

Herald
Press

Scottdale, Pennsylvania
Waterloo, Ontario

Library of Congress Cataloging-in-Publication Data

Vernon, Louise A.
    A heart strangely warmed.

    SUMMARY: An English boy gains a personal acquaintance with John
Wesley whose preachings change his entire life.

    1. Wesley, John, 1703-1791—Juvenile fiction.
[1. Wesley, John, 1703-1791—Fiction. 2. Methodism—Biography—Fiction]
I. Eitzen, Allan, ill. II. Title.
PZ7.V598He [Fic]   75-11767
ISBN 0-8361-1769-7

The paper used in this publication is recycled and meets the minimum re-
quirements of American National Standard for Information Sciences—Per-
manence of Paper for Printed Library Materials, ANSI Z39.48-1984.

To order or request information, please call
1-800-759-4447 (individuals); 1-800-245-7894 (trade).
Website: www.mph.org.

"MY NAME IS
JOHN WESLEY"

Young Robert Upton eased the leather straps of his peddler's tray from his aching shoulders and slumped against the doorway of a London shop. Tears smarted under his eyelids. His first day of peddling and not one sale! Not even a pin or a bit of lace to a London housewife.

What was he going to tell Mother, lying so ill at home?

What would he say to Mrs. Babcock, their busy-body neighbor? He knew he could not return through the little courtyard without her spying on him from her upstairs apartment.

Robert sighed, remembering Mrs. Babcock's shrill disapproval eight days before when Father left London in his new four-wheeled peddler's wagon.

She had exclaimed to all the neighbors, "He's just a junkman. Calls himself a peddler now, does he? He ought to stay home and peddle his cast-off pots and pans in that two-wheeled junk cart of his, the way he has always done. Yes, and keep that sick wife of his home instead of letting her go to those singing prayer meetings in Fetter Lane."

Robert seethed inwardly at the memory. What Mother and Father did was none of Mrs. Babcock's business. In the first place, Mother had insisted on Father's trip. As a traveling peddler, his earnings would be in pounds, rather than shillings and pence. Father needed to make many sales in order to pay for the new wagon with its canvas-covered top. As for her being ill, Mother pointed out that there were plenty of neighbors in the courtyard apartments to help her, as well as the little band of women she had been meeting with lately for prayers and hymn singing. Besides, Robert would be there to help.

A fine help I am, Robert groaned. *Not even one sale.* He adjusted the straps of his tray. For a moment he longed to be once again with Father on the two-wheeled cart calling for cast-offs from London housewives, even though many people jeered at them.

Robert took a deep breath. He had to make a sale somehow. He could not go home without even a penny to show for a day's work.

A small, neatly dressed man hurried up the street. *A gentleman,* Robert decided. But why wasn't he wearing a wig under his three-cornered hat instead of his own shoulder-length hair? And why wouldn't a fine gentleman have silver buckles on his shoes?

6

Robert walked along with the little man. "If you're not in too much of a hurry, sir, I have something to show you."

The little man smiled and stopped. "I am always in haste, but never in a hurry."

What an odd thing to say, Robert thought. *Is there a difference between haste and hurry?* There was no time to think about that now. Robert held out a toy monkey on a string. "A toy for your child, sir?"

The little man blinked and pulled a pair of spectacles from his pocket. *Nearsighted, that's what he is,* Robert decided.

"No, thank you. I have no child."

"A bit of lace for your wife, then?"

The little man smiled sadly. "I have no wife." He started off, but Robert caught up with him.

"A quill pen for yourself?"

"Why, yes. That I shall buy. I do a great deal of writing." He paid for the pen, counting out the coins with care. Then he gave Robert a long and searching look. "What is your name?"

"Robert Upton, sir."

"My name is John Wesley."

Robert looked at John Wesley in astonishment. Why would a gentleman introduce himself to a street peddler? Why had he looked so sad when he said he had no wife? A fine gentleman like John Wesley could find dozens of young women who would be glad to marry him.

"Do you go to church, Robert?"

The totally unexpected question startled Robert. Church? He and Father did not go to church

7

very often. Mother was the churchgoer, even when she did not feel well. *But I can't tell him all that,* Robert thought. Somehow, he sensed John Wesley's personal interest in him.

"I — I go when I can," Robert stammered.

"What have you learned about God?"

John Wesley's penetrating glance bothered Robert, yet he could not turn away from the kind face with its prominent nose and its mouth curved in sweetness. Robert tried to think, but his mind was blank. "Nothing," he said at last. "I have heard some things, but I do not understand them."

"Do you know that your hands and feet, and the rest of your body, will turn to dust in a little while?" John Wesley asked.

Robert tried to think how to answer such a strange question. Dust? There was usually more mud than dust in London, but he knew in a surprising way what John Wesley meant. Such ideas made him uncomfortable. He tried to say *no,* but something within impelled him to say *yes* to John Wesley's question.

"But you will live on. That part of you is called the soul," John Wesley went on.

What baffling talk this was! Who was this man, John Wesley? Did he always ask such questions? Anyway, how could he prove there was such a thing as a soul?

"Can you see it?" Robert asked.

"No. The soul is within you, but you cannot see the wind, either, although it is all about you." John Wesley seemed eager to explain. But he asked another question. "What do you think a soul does?"

Robert strained to think of something to say. "I don't know, sir," he had to admit.

"If you had no soul within you, you could no more see or hear or feel than that stone wall could. What do you think will become of your soul when your body turns to dust?"

What impossible questions John Wesley asked! Robert tugged at the straps of his peddler's tray. "I don't know."

"Why, it will go out of your body into another world and live there always."

Maybe the soul is like the bird, Robert thought. I *wouldn't mind that.* He imagined himself flying above London, above the crowded streets with their coaches, sedan chairs, horsemen, businessmen, and shoppers. That would be fun.

"Do you know who God is?" John Wesley continued.

All at once, Robert burned to get away from the little man and his upsetting questions, but he was held as if in a spell. "No." In his whole life he had never thought about God. Of course he knew God existed. Churches all over London proved it. Most folks went to church at least some of the time, except for people like sailors or thieves, Robert told himself, but how many people really knew God? To his own surprise, he waited in eagerness for John Wesley's answer.

"You cannot see Him any more than you can see your own soul. Yet it is He who made you and me and all men and women, and all beasts and birds, and all the world. It is He who makes the sun shine, the rain fall, and corn and fruits to grow out of the

9

ground. He makes all these for us. But why do you think He made us? What did He make you and me for?"

Another puzzling question! Completely baffled, Robert could only mutter, "I don't know."

"He made you to live with Himself in heaven, and so you will in a little time, if you let Jesus into your life."

Jesus? he asked himself anxiously. Robert always tried to be good. Wasn't that enough? He helped Mother and Father all he could, didn't he? The only bad thing he had done was fight with London street boys when they hooted and jeered at Father's junkman's cart. But all that was over, now that Father was a peddler. No more fights. In talking with John Wesley, Robert felt sure he could be good forever.

A man a little taller than John Wesley hurried up to them. "Pen and ink! Pen and ink!" he called, rubbing his hands. "Brother John, aren't you ever coming home? I've just thought up a new hymn."

"Of course, Brother Charles, I'm coming." With a wave of his hand, John Wesley went off with his brother.

Dazed and unable to shake off the excitement of his encounter with John Wesley, Robert closed his tray and headed for home. He had to tell Mother about the little man. In a hurry, Robert took a shortcut through an unfamiliar street. Suddenly a boy about his own age sprang in front of him. Robert stopped in dismay. He should have known better. Street boys staked out certain areas as their own territory. Street fighting was a way of life in London.

But it was too late to turn back.

"I'm David Elliott." David stood with his feet apart and his fists on his hips. "Who are you?"

For the second time that afternoon, Robert told his name.

"Well, Robert, I want to know what you are doing on my street."

Robert took a cautious stop backward. He knew enough about street fights to know that a leader like David would not stop until he provoked a fight on one pretext or another. A fight would ruin every salable item on Robert's tray. If that happened, how could he help pay for Father's new wagon?

Robert turned to run, but David jumped ahead of him and blocked the way.

"Don't you dare move unless I say so. I asked you what you are doing on my street."

"Going home."

"What's that tray for?"

"Peddling."

David whistled, and several other boys came running. A rising panic choked Robert. He was in for it now. Oh, why had he tried to take a shortcut? Why had he ever met a gentleman named John Wesley? What good was all that talk about God and the soul? It was certainly no help in facing a mob of boys itching for a fight.

"Open up that tray," David commanded.

Aware of the gaze of the semicircle of boys in front of him, Robert fumbled at the snap. David sniffed in scorn at the array of laces, pins, and toys. "Are you trying to sell that junk?"

The word *junk* made Robert wince, but he did not

11

try to defend his wares. "I've made only one sale."

Maybe, just maybe, the boys would let him go.

"What does your father do?" David asked.

"He's a — a merchant." That wasn't quite the truth. Father was a brand-new peddler, but at least Robert would not have to admit Father had been a junk dealer.

David was not satisfied. "A merchant in what line?"

Robert swallowed hard. "Iron."

"You're lying."

"No, I'm not." Father had dealt with iron — people's cast-off pots and pans.

"You'd better tell the truth, or I'll twist your arm."

"He's a peddler."

"I haven't seen a peddler on these streets for a long time. You're lying."

"My father is a traveling peddler." Robert almost wished David would start to fight and get it over with.

One of the boys blurted out, "I've seen him before. His father's a junkman." He started toward Robert with clenched fists. "You're going to pay for lying to us."

To Robert's surprise, David held off the others. "We've got the answer," he shouted.

"Answer to what?" Robert could not help asking.

"We need something to make a noise with."

"What for?" There was enough noise on London streets — coachmen shouting to their horses, the bustle of messengers on foot or horseback, runners carrying sedan chairs, women chatting over their market baskets, and shopkeepers talking to customers.

"We're going to make a lot of noise at a meeting and run off some people who are breaking the law." David seemed friendly now. "Can you get us some old kettles?"

Robert thought of the cast-offs in the stable at home. "Yes, I suppose so."

David turned to the other boys. "We'll all meet tomorrow night across the street from the Fetter Lane place."

Fetter Lane? That was where Mother went to her meetings, Robert realized with a horrible sinking feeling.

"I — I can't get you any kettles," he said in a shaking voice.

David's face darkened. "You just finished saying you could. I'm going home with you. I'll get them myself."

There was no way out. David refused the help of the other boys. "It would cause too much attention. I'll see you tomorrow night at seven."

On the way home, with David close at his side, Robert felt as if he had iron weights on each foot. It was impossible to do as David wanted. On the other hand, it was impossible not to do it.

At the courtyard gate, Robert motioned to David. "In here."

But something had happened to the court. It was filled with people. Women wrung their hands or openly wept. Several men huddled together and talked in low tones. A hearse with four horses and a driver in black cape waited in one corner of the court.

David's face blanched. "I'm not going in there,"

13

he gasped. "Someone has died." He ran off without another word.

A chill ran through Robert. His senses quickened. Something had happened to Mother. He watched four men go into his parents' apartment. There was a bustling at the doorway. The four men, each at the corner of a covered stretcher, walked with measured steps to the hearse. Robert stood utterly still. He did not have to ask. He knew Mother had died.

Mrs. Babcock's shrill voice carried over the murmurs of the neighbors who filled the little court. "I knew it! I warned her! But she insisted on carrying on with that singing and praying group down there in Fetter Lane. Methodists, they call themselves. I told her no good would come of it. 'It's a secret religious meeting,' I told her. 'Such meetings are against the law,' I told her. 'You'll end up either in Bedlam chained to a wall or in Newgate prison.' But would she listen? No. And now God has punished her."

"God have mercy on her soul," a woman cried out.

Anger rose in Robert like fire, pushing at his eardrums, throbbing behind his eyes. God had no mercy. A merciful God would not have taken Mother away. She was kind and good. How happy she had been only a few days ago when Father started his new life as a peddler. Now Mother was dead. Grief would not bring her back. Robert knew that. It was the fault of that Methodist group down there in Fetter Lane breaking the law. What good was all that praying and singing? Those people were just liars, pretending to have God's help when they were really bringing down His wrath. Why hadn't that little man, John Wesley, talked about the God who killed people? All he'd said was a pack of lies.

With tear-blinded eyes, Robert stumbled into the stable and sat on a pile of pots and pans. He knew one thing for sure. Tomorrow night at seven, he would be at the Fetter Lane meeting place of the Methodists with enough noisemakers to scare them from ever meeting again.

Chapter Two

THE
PEOPLE CALLED
METHODISTS

For a long time Robert sat in the stable without moving. What should he do? He didn't want Mrs. Babcock to see him and talk about God punishing Mother with death because she went to those Methodist meetings. He didn't want to see the other neighbors, either, with their hand-wringing and crying. Maybe he could stay in the stable until Father came home.

But what about food? There might be some left-over oatmeal in the apartment. But he couldn't go in there. Not now. He'd slip out to a nearby market before dark and buy food with the money John Wesley had given him for the quill pen.

Outside, two men were talking. Robert recognized the voice of the parish preacher.

"We'll have to send a horseman to find Matthew Upton and tell him about his wife's death," the preacher said.

"But sir, how can we? We don't know where he is," a neighbor replied.

"How long will he be gone?"

"Who knows?"

Robert could almost see the man shrug.

"Didn't he tell anyone?" the preacher asked.

"Maybe his wife."

"Surely he had friends here."

"Well, he kept pretty much to himself. He was just a junkman, you know." The neighbor sounded apologetic.

"Someone said he had a son," the preacher went on.

"Yes, sir. A boy named Robert."

"Of course," the preacher exclaimed. "Now I remember. Robert went to the parish school for several years, then dropped out to help his father. Where is he now?"

"I don't know, sir. No one has seen him all day, and with all the upset over Mrs. Upton's dying, I guess no one thought about him. When he turns up, shall I send him to your house?"

Expecting the preacher to say *yes*, and already feeling a rush of gratitude, Robert almost went outside then, but something held him back.

"No," the preacher said. "I'm afraid we couldn't take him in."

A chill passed through Robert. Why wouldn't the preacher help him? Was it because Father had been a junkman?

17

"You see," the preacher was saying, "Mrs. Upton was attending meetings that I'm afraid were a threat to her soul."

"I've heard some talk about that, sir, but perhaps Mrs. Upton was just a Dissenter. They are within the law, I understand."

"Mrs. Upton was worse than a Dissenter. She was a Methodist."

The loathing with which the preacher uttered the word *Methodist* made Robert squirm. The Methodists must be a terrible group, but if they were, why had Mother gone to their meetings?

The voices died away. After everyone had left the courtyard, Robert darted to the street and headed for the nearest market. With every step he felt more alone. He walked close to the buildings for the comfort of their solid walls. Stories of what could happen to children in London came to his mind. What if people questioned him? How could he prove Father was coming back? People might put him in a workhouse. But that would not be as bad as a prison like Newgate.

The very idea of prison filled Robert with terror. Not that he had ever been in one, but when people lined the streets to watch carts hauling men, women, and children to be hanged at Tyburn, he watched, too. Of course people had to be punished for doing wrong, but it was terrible to think of a child hanged because he'd stolen a handkerchief and a grown-up because he'd stolen forty pence. People like highwaymen who waited around on horseback and robbed travelers — maybe that was different. Or smugglers. Maybe they should be hanged.

Robert tried to put the whole idea out of his mind. He had no intention of doing wrong. *All I have to do is not let anyone I know see me until Father gets back,* he thought. He'd do it, too, without asking help from anyone, or from God either. Robert clenched his fists remembering how God had let Mother die.

At the market Robert bought a loaf of dark bread and tore out a few mouthfuls for his supper. Londoners were homeward bound at this hour. Robert passed a coach-and-four waiting to be hired, its coach number plainly marked on the door. The driver, perched high on the wooden seat, called out, "One shilling, if it's not too long a trip."

"Too expensive," a man called up. "I'll find another."

A hearse came by, drawn by four horses. Robert stared at it in chilled fascination. There was something peculiar about the hearse. True, there were black curtains fluttering at the coach windows, and the driver was dressed in black. But why was he so nervous, bouncing on the high seat, looking over his shoulder constantly with a scowl on his windburned face? Two mourners followed the coach, one a woman holding an open Bible and the other a boy. He looked familiar. David Elliott! The boy who had run away from death that afternoon. What was he doing in a funeral procession acting so calmly?

On second thought, Robert decided David wasn't really calm. David kept looking over his shoulder, too, until the woman nudged him to face forward. The coach-for-hire edged away from the hearse. At the same time, a group of city officials on horseback faced both coaches from the other direction, ready to pass. The horses of both coaches shied and their harnesses tangled.

To Robert's surprise, the woman mourner ran to the driver's seat of the hearse and stepped up. She had on a man's knee breeches and a man's shoes. *The woman was a man.* But why? Robert wanted to ask David, but David had disappeared.

"Let us through," the officials shouted. "We have the right of way."

A crowd gathered to watch.

The driver in black jumped down and frantically untangled the harness. The man-woman held the reins.

"Sirs, where is your respect? This is a hearse."

A sailor called out from the crowd, "A dead body won't mind."

"Get out of the way," an official ordered.

"Sirs, be patient," the man-woman pleaded.

Several sailors near Robert muttered among themselves.

"There's something strange going on," one said.

"Aye. You can say that again," a second replied.

"Were you paid?" asked the first.

"No," the other said with an oath," and I recognize the driver. He's the one who took the goods."

"Well, then, what are we waiting for?"

With a shout the group of sailors crowded around the hearse and began to rock it from side to side.

"Look out! It's going to fall over!" the onlookers yelled.

The crowd backed away and waited in silence. The hearse fell on its side away from the coach-for-hire. The coffin tumbled to the street and splintered open. Horrified cries filled the air, and then cries of amazement. There was no body in the coffin. Instead, parcels of all sizes rolled on the ground.

"It's a smuggler!" someone exclaimed.

An even louder voice declared, "No, it isn't. It's a free trader."

"Free trader! Free trader!" The call passed from person to person. The crowd surged forward, grabbing up packages and scrambling out of the way.

The hearse driver wrung his hands, his windburned face even redder than before. "Sirs! Please! These items have not been priced yet."

But the London onlookers had already ripped open the packages. "Tea!" "French laces!" "Spirits from France!" Those lucky enough to grab a package hurried away with their loot, but the officials grabbed the hearse driver and the man-woman.

"Smugglers," an official said. "They'll feel the weight of the law." He drew an imaginary noose about his neck.

"But it's only free trading," someone in the crowd protested. "Everyone who has the chance does it."

The officials marched the two men away, and Robert listened to the protests of the group who remained.

One man tried to reason with the others. "It's against the English law to free trade. Everyone knows there is a tax on everything that comes here from another shore."

"Tax on imports isn't right," someone objected.

"You must pay Caesar what he is due," the first man said.

21

"What kind of talk is that? There's no one in England called Caesar. Now, if you mean King George — "

"I meant King George. Caesar was just another name."

"Well, it isn't right. Pay for something once, and that should be all. Taxes, taxes, taxes. They'll be the death of England and all free trade."

Loud laughter greeted this remark. Robert started home, tired out. He stayed close to the buildings again. At the doorway of a shop he almost stumbled over David Elliott, sitting with head down and knees to his chin.

"David?" Robert questioned in a shocked whisper. He had seen two different Davids that afternoon — one who had challenged Robert with cocksure defiance, and one who had run in fear from something he could not handle. The David here in the doorway sat shriveled in dejection. *I know just how he feels,* Robert thought.

"Was that man your father?" he asked.

David shook his head. "It was my uncle. I don't have a father."

"Aren't you going to go home and tell your mother what happened?"

"I don't have a mother."

"Then you can stay with me," Robert blurted.

David jumped up, his eyes sparkling.

"We can stay in the apartment," Robert went on, but his words were drowned out by the rumble of a wagon on the street behind him.

David's face blanched. He clutched Robert's arm. "We've got to hide."

22

"Their men pick up children from the streets. They make you work for them until you die," David said.

Robert looked back into the street. A wagonload of children headed their way. "Why do we have to hide? What's the matter?"

David pulled Robert into a shadowed nook. "It's the mills. Their men pick up children from the streets. They make you work for them until you die. But they're not going to catch us."

The boys huddled in the shadows, hardly breathing. The wagon creaked to a halt not far away.

"Cadwallader, how many do we have now?" Robert heard a man ask.

"There are supposed to be fifteen," Cadwallader replied.

"*Supposed* to be? Don't you know? Count them again," the first man ordered.

"Only fourteen," Cadwallader reported after a moment.

"Where's the other one? Find out if he's here."

"Who, sir?" Cadwallader asked.

"Why, the fifteenth."

"What's his name?"

"How would I know his name?" the first man said in an angry tone.

"Then I can't very well call for him," Cadwallader said.

"Cadwallader, don't these children have names?"

"Not that I know of. They don't last long in the mills, you know."

"I know," the first man said. "Really, it's a pity. Still, they don't grow up to be thieves and hang on Tyburn Hill."

"That's true," Cadwallader said.

"We need another child to fill the quota."

"I thought I saw one back there," Cadwallader replied.

"Go see."

David sprang to his feet. "Run!"

Both boys ran down the street. David ducked into an alley and Robert followed. They emerged on another street right into the arms of two young men.

"Whoa, there, boys. Where are you going so fast?" one laughed.

"They're trying to catch us for the mills."

"Not if we can help it," the second young man said. "You boys stay with us and we'll take care of you."

Robert noted that the young men were not gentlemen. Both were dressed in dark knee breeches and slightly flared waistcoats. Underneath their three-cornered hats they wore their own hair instead of a wig.

"Where are your parents?" one of the young men asked.

Robert spoke up for both himself and David. "They're — they're not here."

"You're alone here in London?"

Robert could tell that David was not going to mention his uncle's arrest. *And I can't say anything about Father because I don't know when he's coming back,* he thought. He nodded in answer to the young man's question.

The young man turned to his companion. "This is just what we were talking about in our little society. It isn't enough to bring the message of free salvation to sinners."

"That's true," the other agreed with enthusiasm.

25

"This afternoon when we were at Newgate with the condemned prisoners, I was thinking all the time how their souls might have been saved years ago if they had been properly guided when they were young."

Robert listened with growing uneasiness. That word, *soul.* Wasn't that what John Wesley had talked about?

"Yes, I'll never forget those prisoners. It was as if they were dying of thirst. How they drank in the Word of God."

Robert stared at the men. How could they be so happy talking about God. Didn't they know God was cruel, unjust, and unmerciful? Didn't they know God killed innocent people like Mother?

"And to think people are ready here in London, and all over England, for news of salvation. George Whitefield has already proved it with the miners up there in Bristol."

The first man patted Robert on the shoulder. "We can start right here in London with these two boys."

"What are you going to do with us?" Robert asked in alarm.

"We are hoping to gather together a group of boys like you two that we can train."

"For the mills?"

The young man smiled. "Certainly not. You will learn a trade so that you can earn your own living, but more important, you will learn God's will for you."

"But I don't want to learn God's will for me," Robert exclaimed. "Do you, David?"

David's face showed suspicion and a growing fear.
"No, and let's not stay here any longer."

"But boys, we just want to help you."

With a yell of terror, David jerked away. "You're
— you're *Methodists*. You're worse than the mills."

He bolted down the street. Robert twisted away
from the young men and followed David. The
Methodists were not going to get either of them.

Chapter Three

THE
NEW FAITH

With David in the lead, Robert ran through twisting London streets until he thought his lungs would burst. David slowed down and Robert caught up with him. "Are you going home with me?" he panted.

"Are there any Methodists there?" David asked with a flash of his old spirit. He grinned, sure of himself again.

Was this the same David who had been so afraid only a few minutes ago?

"No. There aren't any Methodists where I live," Robert said. Mrs. Babcock wasn't one, not the way she had shouted about Mother.

At the courtyard, David stopped at the gate. "Who died here today?"

"My mother."

28

Once again David changed. His eyes widened. "Aren't you afraid to go into that apartment now?"

David's uncertainty made Robert bold. "Why should I be afraid?" It wasn't necessary to mention that if David had not been there, Robert would have stayed in the stable until Father returned. "We have to eat. There's a sack of oats inside. We can make some oatmeal for supper." Robert had a sudden memory of a loaf of bread he had bought. Where was it? He could not remember where, how, or when it had been jostled out of his arms by the crowd. It did not matter now. With David here, Robert was not afraid to go into the apartment.

Later, after, Robert and David each finished two bowls of hot oatmeal, they sat before the fireplace. Robert thought of all that had happened that day. He tried not to think of Mother. Much better to think about the Methodists and how much he hated them.

"What do you know about them?" he asked.

David pretended ignorance. "Who?"

David's bland expression did not fool Robert. "The Methodists. You knew what I meant."

"How would I know unless you speak out? Yes, I know all about them. My Uncle Jem told me."

"What does the word mean?"

Again David pretended he did not know what Robert meant. "What word?" he asked in mock innocence.

Robert grew impatient. "You know what word I mean. *Methodists*."

"Well," David began in a rush, then stopped, his

29

face amusingly blank. "They're people who use a — that is, they have a method."

"Method?" Somehow the word had no meaning at all for Robert. It wasn't a word like *horse*, or *cart*, or *bread*, a word you could see, touch, or taste.

"Well, it means they use a — they have a — they do things in a certain way." David was becoming annoyed. "What's the matter? You stupid or something?"

"No. I just want to know what *Methodist* means."

David sighed. "All right, then. I'll tell you what my Uncle Jem told me about them. He used to work for an Oxford man who was there when all this started. It was a holy club. Everyone had to get up at four and pray until five and then they would go out and help people."

"I help Father," Robert said. "Is that a method?"

"Of course not. You do it because you have to." Methodists do things for God."

God was a word Robert did not want to hear. Nevertheless, something prompted his next question in spite of himself. "Do you believe in God?"

David glared at Robert and sputtered, "Well, I — well, yes, I suppose so. Don't you?"

Taken aback, Robert tried to sift his thoughts. He had to believe the God who took Mother's life. How could He be the God who *gave* us life, the way that little man John Wesley had said? How could one believe in both?

"Do you or don't you?" David was saying.

"I guess I believe in God," Robert said with reluctance. "I'm afraid not to," he added in a rush.

"You ought to become a Methodist," David

30

teased. "They're afraid, too, my uncle says. That's why they sing and pray so much. Uncle Jem says he knows a man who wore a hole in the ground by a tree where he prayed so much. Methodists believe in such crazy things. They thank God for everything that happens. If someone doesn't pay back money he owes, you're supposed to give thanks. Or if you have nothing to eat but a leaf of lettuce, give thanks."

Should I give thanks because Mother died? Robert thought. *Never!* Aloud, he asked, "Why do Methodists believe such strange things?"

"My uncle says they think God is more willing to do things for people than they have allowed Him to do, but they have to be more thankful first and then let Him guide them."

Somehow the idea of thankfulness stayed with Robert that night, even though he tried not to think about it. The next morning David shook Robert awake. "There's someone at the door. It's a man."

The door opened. "Father!" Robert shouted, flinging himself in his father's arms. "How did you know about Mother?

Father said a strong inner urge prompted him to return home. Friends had already met him and told him about Mother. Father brooded a moment. "In a strange way, I already knew." He seemed to notice David for the first time. "Who is your friend?"

"David Elliott."

"I know a man named Elliott — Jem Elliott."

"He's my uncle."

"I bought some goods from him for my trip."

Robert's head pounded with a sudden sickening

31

pulse. Father did not know the goods had been smuggled. He could be arrested. *Shall I tell him about Jem Elliott's arrest?* David's warning glance told Robert to be careful.

"Can David stay here with us? He doesn't have a mother, and his uncle has — gone away."

"Of course he can stay, as long as he likes." Father left to make the funeral arrangements. When he came back, Mrs. Babcock from upstairs came in with him. She did not rant about the Methodists to Father, Robert noticed, but talked quietly about the funeral.

Robert saw a change in Father. What could have happened? Mrs. Babcock seemed to notice it, too.

"You are so calm, Mr. Upton. How is it possible in the face of this terrible tragedy?"

Father motioned everyone to sit down. "There was this little man, a gentleman, you could tell that soon enough, even though he wore his own hair instead of a wig. He was talking to some people when I was coming by, and there something about the way he talked that I can't forget. Such a strange thing it was."

"Do go on," Mrs. Babcock said.

"I can't shake off his words. He said, 'Examine yourselves, whether you be in the faith.' He talked about the Apostle Paul saying, 'If any man be in Christ, he is a new creature. Old things have passed away. Behold, all things have become new.' "

Robert listened, puzzled. He had never heard Father talk about such things before, but Robert could guess who the little man was.

"I would like to hear this man," Mrs. Babcock exclaimed. "Who is he?"

"I don't know. No one mentioned his name."

"It's John Wesley," Robert blurted. David looked at him in astonishment.

Mrs. Babcock jumped up, her eyes blazing. "What! So that's the man you heard. He's one of the false prophets spoken of in Scripture. How can you be taken in by the falsehoods he speaks? I'll not stay here and listen to another word."

She bustled out muttering her indignation. "I've a good mind to report this," Robert thought he heard her say.

Father had to take care of other details. He sent the boys to the blacksmith with the horse. "Have him tighten her loose shoe," he told them. When the boys came back, later than they had expected, Mrs. Babcock in the overhead apartment pushed open the shutters and leaned on the ledge with folded arms. The look on her face told Robert she knew something he did not want to hear. David noticed it, too.

"What is she up to?" he whispered.

Mrs. Babcock called down, "Your father is not home. Took him away, they did, hardly a quarter of an hour ago. The church clock had just struck."

"Took him away? Who? Where?"

"The *who* is the law, and the *where* is the jail. Now he's with the other one."

Robert echoed her again. "The other one?"

"Yes, the one they call Jem Elliott. Oh, I found out all about it, how that hearse hauled smuggled goods and how those sailors tipped it over and allowed justice to take place. Not only that, but justice caught up with your father, too. Serves him right. If he had stayed a junkman the way God intended, he wouldn't be in jail now." Mrs. Babcock ducked back inside and closed the shutters.

David picked up a stone and started to throw it. Robert caught his arm. "No, don't do that, David. It won't help."

Nothing helped. Once again burning thoughts of anger churned in Robert's mind. *Why had God permitted this to happen? Father would not have knowingly bought smuggled goods. With Father in jail, what would he and David do? How would we live? On the streets, like many other children? Would we be caught and put in the workhouse or the mills?*

After a supper of oatmeal, David said, "It's just what Uncle Jem said. Those Methodists have started all the trouble."

Robert could not see how the Methodists had anything to do with Father being in jail, but he was ready to believe anything.

"How?" he asked.

"Because they've made so many people dissatisfied, that's how. Going around praying and singing the way they do is enough to bother people." David straightened up. "I almost forgot," he said in awe. "Tonight's the night. Come on. Let's get moving. The other boys will be there. Where are the kettles?"

For a second Robert did not remember what David was talking about. Then he remembered David's scheme, jumped up, and grabbed David's arm. Action! That's what Robert wanted. The Methodists were to blame, he tried to convince himself. If they had stayed home minding their own business, Mother would never have gone to their meetings and got drenched in the rain and then fallen ill. None of the terrible things would have followed, and he would be home safe with Mother and Father right now.

Robert led the way to the stable. He pounded one kettle after another with long battered spoons trying them out for sound until David told him to be quiet.

"Wait until we get to Fetter Lane. Do you want Mrs. Babcock to hear us?"

"No," Robert agreed. He helped David carry the kettles to the street. "I don't think she'll see us now that it's dark."

At Fetter Lane, Robert and David waited for the other boys. Already the singing had begun across the street.

"They'd better hurry," Robert grumbled. He was ready to make enough noise to raise the dead. He winced. He hadn't meant to think such words. What would Mother think if she were alive and knew what mischief he was up to? Oh, it was mischief, all right. Robert knew enough about right and wrong to realize that.

"Remember, it's against the law to have more than five people meeting together like this," David reminded him. "Uncle Jem told me all about it."

The singing across the street became louder. It sounded vigorous and joyful. In spite of himself, Robert had to admit he liked it.

The other boys came up one by one. David handed out kettles and spoons. "The minute they stop singing, we'll go across the street and start pounding on the kettles."

Robert felt more and more uneasy. "What do you think they'll do?"

"Why, they'll give up and go home. That's what my uncle says they ought to do. He says they should be chained like the crazy people in Bedlam or put in Newgate prison and then taken to Tyburn and hanged."

Once again assured that the Methodists were troublemakers, Robert waited for the signal. The singing stopped.

David called, "Now." He led the way across the street.

The boys banged the iron kettles with all their might.

"Run back and forth," David ordered. "Make them think there's an army out here."

Robert pounded with every ounce of strength he had. He pounded out his hurt, his anger, his grief, his despair, his protest to the God who ran the world the way He did. Robert felt a kind of delirious joy in seeing how much noise he could make. He'd pound all night long or at least until something happened.

Something did happen. There was a stir at the door of the meeting place.

"They're coming out. Run!" David commanded. He was off in a flash, the other boys at his heels. Robert, still in a daze, was too slow. A man caught him by the collar.

"Here's one of them."

"Who is it?" someone called out.

Robert pounded with every ounce of strength he had, protesting
the way God ran the world.

"Why, it's Robert Upton, the junk dealer's son," a woman gasped.

Robert flinched. The words *junk dealer* sounded as if Father was a criminal.

"Poor lad. His mother just died yesterday. Poor, motherless boy."

Her pity was worse than the other's scorn.

"What are we going to do with him?"

"Let Mr. Wesley handle it," someone suggested.

The group parted. Robert looked up into the hurt, questioning eyes of John Wesley, the little man who had told him about God.

He remembers me, Robert realized. The disappointment in John Wesley's eyes went straight to Robert's heart. He had wronged the man who was only trying to help him understand God's ways.

With a gasp of shame, Robert whirled, plunged through the circle of people, and for the second time in two days ran away from the Methodists.

AN
INVITATION
FROM BRISTOL

Shouts of "Wait!" spurred Robert to run faster. In the darkness he stumbled over a kettle one of the other boys had flung aside in flight. Robert sprawled headlong and tried to spring to his feet. A sharp pain in his ankle convinced him that there was no use trying to outrun the Methodists. He rubbed his ankle and watched the lanterns of the group approach him.

"Were they all boys?" he heard someone ask, as if surprised.

"Yes," he heard John Wesley say. "Some were bareheaded, some barefooted, and barelegged."

Robert winced at the man's quiet good humor. He just could not face the little preacher. With both hands, Robert hoisted himself up, took a hesitant step, and winced again. He was as good as chained on the spot, and with one fleeting glance toward Wesley, Robert stared at his ankle.

"Why do you look as if you'd never seen me before?" John Wesley asked.

"Oh, sir, I'm sorry," Robert blurted, and to his surprise found himself telling about Mother dying and Father being put in jail.

"What for?" someone asked.

"Uh — free trading," Robert said.

"That's smuggling," someone gasped.

"A detestable practice," John Wesley said. "May our Lord bid your father's chains to fall off."

"But, sir," Robert burst out, "my father is an honest man. He would never have bought the goods if he had known they were smuggled." To Robert's joy, he saw that Wesley believed him.

John Wesley arranged to have some of the Methodists visit the jail the next day. As for Robert's sprained ankle, Wesley advised, "Mix a little turpentine with flour and the yolk of an egg. Apply it as a plaster."

Such advice surprised several of the Methodists. "Mr. Wesley, are you a doctor as well as a preacher?" one asked.

John Wesley shook his head. "No, but it is my design some day to set down cheap, safe, and simple medicines, easily obtained and applied by plain men."

"But you *are* a healer," someone insisted. "I have heard it said elsewhere."

"You are thinking of my Uncle Matthew," John Wesley said. "I am a healer of the soul."

"Yes, that you are. Let's go back to the meeting-house and continue our service."

"A good idea," John Wesley agreed.

But just then someone called, "Here's another one of those boys." Several Methodists held up their lanterns.

His face set with determination, David came to Robert's side.

"Why did you come back? You didn't have to," Robert whispered.

David's sheepish grin answered him. David was not going to let his new friend down.

"I think these boys should join with us in prayer and song before we let them go," someone suggested, after learning David's name.

"Aren't they going to punish us?" David whispered in surprise.

David's astonishment touched Robert's funny bone. He laughed hysterically, which in turn touched off David. Neither boy could stop. The friendliness of the Methodists turned into sternness, but John Wesley showed sympathy. In the meeting room a little later, when everyone had settled down, he spoke of an experience he and his brother shared at Oxford.

"I used to be surprised at those who were tempted by Satan to laugh so hard they could hardly quit. I could scarcely believe their account until I had the same experience ten or eleven years ago. My brother Charles and I used to spend part of Sunday walking in the fields and singing. One day, just as we were beginning to sing, he burst out laughing. At first I was angry, but then I began to

41

laugh as loud as he. We couldn't have stopped if we tried. We weren't able to sing another line."

John Wesley had a way of explaining things with simple words and quiet authority. Robert felt better about everything that had happened. Even his ankle had quit throbbing.

In the meeting someone questioned the experience of conversion. "I don't believe it can happen as fast as some people say."

Robert looked at David. Here was another word, *conversion,* as hard to understand as the word *Methodist,* but of course now he understood something about the *method* of the Methodists. What happened to people who were converted?

John Wesley explained his own experience. Whenever he and his brother Charles needed guidance, they opened the Bible to see what God would tell them. On May 24 the year before, at about five in the morning, he had opened his Bible to 2 Peter 1:4 and read, "Whereby are given unto us exceeding great and precious promises: that by these ye might be partakers of the divine nature." He flipped the pages again and read Mark 12:34, "Thou art not far from the kingdom of God."

John Wesley explained how he had gone to a society in Aldersgate Street. Someone was reading Luther's preface to the Epistle to the Romans, describing the change which God works in the heart through faith in Christ.

"I felt my heart strangely warmed," Wesley said. "An assurance was given me that He had taken away my sins and saved me from the law of sin and death."

Robert believed what the little man said. *But things like that don't have anything to do with me,* he thought.

"Then if you are converted, you do not have any more problems?" someone asked.

John Wesley smiled. "I have found more and more that a Christian is always at war with sin. We need to watch and pray lest we enter into temptation."

A stunned silence met his remark. "But I thought conversion meant your life became more peaceful," someone ventured.

John Wesley told how he had returned home on May 24, after his heart had been strangely warmed. "I was battered with temptations. They returned again and again. But as I lifted up my eyes to God He sent me help from His holy place. The difference between this and my former life is that then I was often conquered. Now I am always conqueror as long as I keep my eye fixed on Him. This is the peace that passes all understanding."

Peace did not mean just quietness, Robert discovered. When John Wesley introduced a new hymn written by his brother Charles, everyone sang it with gusto. Robert joined in, too, pleased to discover he had a good voice. David at first ducked his head, but when he heard the chorus of the song for the fourth time, he sang with the others. Robert could see by David's grin that he enjoyed the singing of the Methodists.

Afterward, outside, a curious passerby asked one of the Methodists, "What is this group?"

"A Church of England Religious Society," the Methodist answered.

"Oh, part of the Church of England, is it?"

"Yes. Would you like to visit us next Wednesday?"

The passerby seemed reluctant. "Are you sure a meeting like this is lawful?"

"This society is part of the Church of England," the Methodist said again. "The leader of our society is an ordained preacher."

"Who is the leader?"

"John Wesley."

The passerby exclaimed in horror and scurried away.

Why were people afraid of Methodists? Robert asked himself, not yet ready to go home and leave these friendly people who seemed to have forgotten about the earlier noisemaking.

A newcomer to the group asked John Wesley what Methodists believed.

"We believe that all Scripture is given by the inspiration of God," John Wesley explained, "and that the written Word of God is the only and sufficient rule both of Christian faith and practice." He added, "As for opinions which do not strike at the root of Christianity, we think and let think."

The newcomer had another question. "I understand that you are part of the Church of England, but what about the *method* you follow?"

In his clear, ringing voice, John Wesley made the method perfectly plain. "Do all the good you can, by all the means you can, in all the ways you can, in all the places you can, at all the times you can, to all the people you can, as long as ever you can."

The word *method* made sense to Robert now.

"Then why are people afraid of the Methodists?"
he asked David on the way home. "There is
nothing to be afraid of."

"Well, why did you run so fast yesterday?"
David teased.

Robert could not answer, but he knew that question would be with him for a long time. How was
it possible that a method for following the Word of
God could frighten people? Then he remembered
Mother, lying dead. Did God punish people because
they didn't believe? But John Wesley believed, and
now some people were afraid of him and his method
Why?

At the courtyard, Robert saw candlelight gleam-
ing from the front window of the Upton apartment.
He clutched David's arm. "Someone's in there."

"What shall we do? Do you think it's a robber?"

"There isn't much to steal," Robert said. "Maybe it's just Mrs. Babcock. She always has to know
everything that goes on."

"But what could go on in an empty apartment?"

"Come on. Let's peek in the window." Robert
led the way. When he looked through the window he
saw a man sitting by the fire.

"It's your father," David exclaimed.

With a whoop of joy, Robert raced inside, hardly
noticing his throbbing ankle.

"Where have you boys been?" Father thundered.

"But you were in jail, Father."

Father looked blank. "In jail? What is that all
about?"

It took some time to unscramble the misunder-
standings.

45

"Mrs. Babcock said so," Robert began, and then blurted out what he and David had done to the Methodists, and how good the Methodists had been to them. He could not help smiling at the changes of expression on Father's face, from frowns to smiles.

In his turn, Father told how he had gone to see Jem Elliott at the prison to make sure the goods he had bought were not smuggled. "By a miracle, they were honest goods, honestly bought and sold."

"Will they let Uncle Jem out of prison?" David asked with hope in his voice.

"I'm afraid there are too many counts against him for real smuggling," Father said. "But remember, David, you're staying with us now, and since both you boys seem well on the way to becoming good Methodists, you can go to the meetings with me." He continued with a sigh, "But let's try to keep out of the way of Mrs. Babcock."

A FEW DAYS later, after the funeral service for Mother, Robert, his father, and David went to a meeting of the religious society in Fetter Lane. This time, instead of peaceful unity, the meeting broke out in arguments.

"I don't think he should go," one man stated.

"Nor I," others echoed.

"George Whitefield has no right to take him away from us," the first man went on. "Let Whitefield stay in Bristol, and let the Wesley brothers stay here where they belong."

It took Robert a little while to learn what had disturbed everyone. George Whitefield, the preacher in Bristol, had written to John Wesley asking him to come to Bristol right away to carry on the work of converting the many people there who hungered for news of salvation.

In the Fetter Lane group, some believed he should go and others fought the idea.

"His brother Charles can hardly bear the mention of Bristol," a man remarked. "Charles Wesley says he might not survive his brother's going there."

"True," another said. "I heard Charles Wesley remark, 'I look with envy on a corpse.' He's sick after every meal because of the hardships he suffered in America."

"John Wesley suffered them too," a third man put in. "He was in America with Charles, you know."

"Why they went to Georgia I'll never understand," a woman said. "Those savages! Nothing was more distasteful, more foreign to their habits. Why did they go there?"

"Because John Wesley was more interested in saving Indians than in saving himself," someone said.

"Why did Charles go?"

"He went because his brother wished it."

Robert listened to the talk, hoping John Wesley would not go to Bristol. He wanted to hear more from this man about how to live a better life. Yes, and about God, too, and even about conversion, although Robert did not think such an experience was necessary for him or for David. Maybe it was for Father. But most of all, Robert wanted to be near John Wesley.

The people continued arguing for and against

Wesley going to Bristol. At last, when no agreement could be reached, John Wesley opened the Bible for guidance. He placed his finger on a passage and read aloud from Ezekiel 24:16, "Son of man, behold, I take away from thee the desire of thine eyes with a stroke: yet neither shalt thou mourn nor weep, neither shall thy tears run down."

Charles Wesley put his head in his hands and did not say another word. Others exclaimed in awe. Robert felt an invisible Force in the room, like the wind John Wesley had mentioned the first time Robert met him.

"If you go, you'll never return alive," a woman said through her tears.

"My life probably is nearly finished," John Wesley told the group.

Another woman burst into tears. "Oh, don't say such a thing."

Charles Wesley made a request. "Let me go, too, so I can die with him."

At this point, everyone agreed that Charles must not leave them. Fetter Lane needed a strong leader, and if John Wesley had to go, one of the brothers should stay behind. And so it was agreed that John Wesley would go to Bristol.

"When?" someone asked.

"Tomorrow."

Robert swallowed hard at this news. He had come to the meeting of the Methodists to hear this little man, and now John Wesley was leaving London.

When will I ever see him again? he wondered in despair.

Chapter Five

PLAIN TRUTH
FOR PLAIN PEOPLE

The next morning when Robert and David went outside, Father had almost filled the wagon with goods to sell.

Robert tried to keep his voice steady. "Are you going away again?"

Father smiled. "How would you and David like to go to Bristol?"

"Bristol? That's where John Wesley is going," David blurted.

"I know. If we hurry, we may be in Bristol almost as soon as he is."

Robert let out a whoop of joy. David's grin spread almost to his ears.

"You boys roll up the bedclothes. We may have to sleep in the wagon — or under it."

The picture became clear to Robert. "We can sell things in Bristol and earn our living."

"Yes, and hear John Wesley preach," Father said.

Since meeting John Wesley, Father had changed. Robert could not have explained how, but there was no time to think about it. He had to help David make a peddler's tray like his own.

When they were ready to leave, Mrs. Babcock ran out into the courtyard to tell them good-bye. Robert stared at her in astonishment. Was this the same Mrs. Babcock they had always known? This woman spoke soft words instead of harsh ones. She apologized to Father for her previous criticisms and volunteered to look after the apartment while they were gone. "God be with you," she murmured.

What had happened to Mrs. Babcock?

"She met John Wesley and was converted," Father explained later.

"But how could she change so fast?"

"Conversion can happen in an instant. Afterward, you see things differently. I know."

So Father had experienced conversion, too! Even after they were well on the way, with Robert and David on the front seat of the wagon with Father, Robert still puzzled over the new and likable Mrs. Babcock and the strange experience called *conversion*.

"When did you meet Mr. Wesley?" Robert asked Father.

"In Oxford." Father thought a moment. "I was too busy to listen."

"Oh, when you were peddling."

"Yes. I was near the castle at the time, and Mr.

Wesley had just finished preaching to the prisoners there."

David leaned forward. "You mean he talks to prisoners?"

Robert knew what David was thinking. What if — what if some day Mr. Wesley came back to London and talked to David's Uncle Jem. Could a criminal be converted?

"Anyone can be converted," Father said. "It's God's plan for everybody."

As the wagon jogged along, Father told how John Wesley and his brother Charles prayed and preached and sang to the condemned prisoners at Newgate prison. Some of the prisoners repented. When the day of execution came, John and Charles Wesley climbed into the death cart with the prisoners and prayed all the way to the gallows. The crowds who always gathered to watch prisoners die were astonished to see some go to their death praising God.

"Do you mean a person can die and still be saved?" David's expression of both hope and disbelief made Robert smile. "But *how?*"

"I don't know how," Father admitted.

Robert remembered his first talk with John Wesley. "I know, Father. Everyone has a body and a soul. You can't see the soul any more than you can see the wind, but it's there, and it lives after you die. That's what Mr. Wesley said."

Father agreed, and urged the horse to a faster pace, as if to reach Bristol even before Mr. Wesley arrived on horseback. But the loaded wagon did not go fast. Later, Father hired a second horse at a farmhouse. Even so, with several stops in villages for peddling, it was several days before Robert, his father, and David reached the sloping streets of Bristol. "This is the second largest seaport in England," Father told the boys, "and famous for its mines."

He questioned a man on the street. "Do you know where John Wesley preaches?"

"John Wesley? Never heard of him."

Several more gave the same answer. A little later a man heard the name *John Wesley* and glared at Father. "Do you mean the man who is taking George Whitefield's place?"

Father nodded.

The man thumped his cane on the cobblestones. "I suppose he'll use George Whitefield's pulpit," he roared.

"Where is his pulpit?"

"Any place and every place — on a wall, in the streets and highways, or in the fields." The man brandished his cane. "Most of the churches here won't let him preach inside."

"It's the same here as in London," Father told the boys later. "I heard Mr. Wesley himself say that he and his brother were not permitted to preach in most of the churches in London."

Another passerby grew red in the face at the mention of John Wesley's name. "It is useless to hope that Mr. Wesley can undo the harm that has been done to Bristol through this field preaching of Mr. Whitefield. Five thousand workingmen have been turned from their daily work. If this Mr. Wesley preaches to the Kingswood miners, I foresee an enormous increase in the price of coal."

At last Father found a man who responded with enthusiasm to his questions. "If John Wesley has a voice you can hear, he will have hundreds of listeners out in the fields."

Robert tried to imagine what it would be like for a man to preach in the open air.

"Now, you take Mr. Whitefield," the man went on. "When he speaks, you can hear him for a mile. When he sings, you can hear him for two." "George Whitefield is one of us," he added. "He's the son of a stableman, you know, but he got into Oxford University by his own efforts."

These words awakened a new kind of hunger in Robert. He knew that gentlemen like Mr. Wesley went to college and learned all there was to know. But how did an ordinary person like Mr. Whitefield go to college? *By his own efforts,* the man on the street had said. It wasn't enough to be able to read a little and to know enough arithmetic to make change for people when they bought something out of his peddler's tray, Robert decided. He wanted to go to school again. But how was that possible, now that he and David were traveling with Father? Still, listening to Mr. Wesley would be an education in itself.

Father asked the man where the religious society met.

"Oh, there are several bands that Mr. Whitefield started." The man counted them off on his fingers. "One meets in Nicholas Street, and one in Baldwin Street. Then of course there's Weavers' Hall, Castle Street, Gloucester Lane, and Back Lane."

Robert groaned. "How do we know where Mr. Wesley will be?"

That evening he and David went with Father to the Baldwin Street society. There were so many people in the yard and at the entrance that Robert could see there was no chance of getting inside. People were talking about Mr. Whitefield leaving.

"Yes, I followed him this afternoon to Bowling Green, Hanham Mount, and Rose Green," a man said. "I counted twenty-four coaches. Imagine! Wealthy people coming to hear an outdoor preacher."

"Too bad the wind kept his voice from carrying well," another remarked.

"But his voice was strong, very strong."

A man with a hearty voice in back of Robert asked to make his way to the door.

"That's Mr. Whitefield," several exclaimed.

Robert turned and saw a man with a slight squint and cheerful, open face. From all sides people wished him well. Women wept. The press of people was so great Mr. Whitefield could not make headway through them. Someone brought a ladder. Mr. Whitefield climbed up and went over the roof of the adjoining house before he could get to the door.

In his farewells he kept telling people, "I leave my dear and honored friend, Mr. Wesley, to confirm those who are awakened."

"Where is Mr. Wesley now?" someone called.

"Preaching at the Nicholas Street society."

Someone near Robert was critical. "Your John Wesley is too high class. He preaches only to the rich."

"That's not true," a woman retorted.

"I suppose you'll say he preaches to the poor then."

"No, he preaches to the working man."

"I don't think he'll be like George Whitefield and take to field preaching."

Another man broke in. "Well, if he ever needs a barn to preach in, I'll let him use mine if he'll fix it up and let me have the front pew for the rest of my life."

Others wondered how John Wesley would like preaching in fields and having an audience of Kingswood miners whose faces remained grimy no matter how hard they tried to clean them.

The next day Robert learned that George Whitefield had laid the cornerstone for a school for the miners in Kingswood. At four that afternoon, Robert stood with Father and David on a little slope near Bristol and heard John Wesley preach to hundreds of people.

"The Spirit of the Lord is upon me," Wesley said. "He has anointed me to preach the gospel to the poor. He has sent me to heal the brokenhearted, to preach deliverance to the captives, and recovering of sight to the blind, to set at liberty those who are bruised."

"John Wesley's right when he says he speaks the plain truth for plain people," Father commented. He planned a schedule for Robert, David, and himself so that they could all attend as many of John Wesley's meetings as possible. Each boy took a peddler's tray and combed the streets and marketplaces on his own for sales.

Robert soon discovered that Bristol knew John

Wesley was there. Many people actually hungered for salvation. But those who didn't want any part of the plain truth from the Bible grumbled.

At one of the meetings, a blacksmith complained about John Wesley's influence. "We should drive him away. He's breaking up family life."

"How is that?" Father asked.

"My wife used to mind her own business, but now she insists on coming to these meetings all the time."

"Doesn't she cook your meals anymore?"

"Well, yes, she does that," the man admitted.

"Does she keep the house clean, your clothes mended, and look after the children?"

"I have to admit she does."

"What else would you have her do for you?" Father asked.

The blacksmith scratched his head. "I just don't like these ideas she's got."

To Robert's surprise, the blacksmith was one of the first ones converted, and in an instant, too, just as Father had said.

David had been watching the blacksmith, along with everyone else during the prayers and singing, and Robert knew just how puzzled he felt.

"What happened to him?" David whispered. "I mean what went on inside of him?"

Robert shook his head. "I don't know, but some day maybe we both will find out."

The next week Robert, Father, and David spent the night in Kingswood and went to the nearest church on Sunday. A group of miners came to the churchyard, their faces and clothes grimy from the coal mines.

"What are these people doing here?" the minister roared.

"Why, sir, these are the miners," his assistant answered. "They've always lived here, and now with the rebirth of religious feeling through Mr. Whitefield — "

"Then let Mr. Whitefield take care of them," the minister said.

"But, sir, he has left, and now Mr. Wesley has awakened many."

"Then let Mr. Wesley take care of them. These people don't belong to my parish."

The assistant wrung his hands. "But, sir, what are we to do? The Lord's Supper has begun. Are we to deny them?"

"Don't criticize me," the minister retorted. "Send them away."

How puzzling, Robert thought. Why should miners be turned away from God?

The miners muttered among themselves. "If he'll not have us, I know one who will," one declared.

"Yes, George Whitefield. But he went away."

"But another preacher is taking his place. John Wesley is his name."

"Then we'll hear him."

"Where is he?"

"At Hanham Mount."

"We'll go there."

Robert looked at Father, who asked directions from someone, motioned the boys to follow, and started off.

At Hanham Mount they joined hundreds of people, most of them miners.

"Ho, everyone who thirsts. Come to the waters,"

John Wesley told them. An eager silence enveloped the crowd.

"You have a Friend here," John Wesley went on. "He stands beside you."

The miners stared at each other in puzzlement.

"He is with you night and day."

There was a rustle like a soft wind among the miners. Some of them shifted from one foot to another. Others coughed.

"He never leaves you. You can turn to Him anytime, day or night."

Everyone waited. No one moved.

"Does this Friend bring you money if you have none? Does He bring you grain, if you have none? No, but He inspires the hearts of those who can supply your needs."

Several miners grunted approval.

"Does this Friend force His way on you?" John Wesley continued. "No. You have to ask first." Wesley invited anyone who felt God's presence to speak up.

Robert could see that no one was quite ready to talk, but most of the hundreds of people drank in Wesley's words as if they were the water of life.

"The new minister speaks plain," Robert heard someone say afterward.

Later he found out that when John Wesley was at Oxford he tried out his sermons on a girl without much education. Each time she could not understand, she would interrupt.

"Let's answer sometime," David suggested.

"Answer what?" Robert stalled, just as David had done weeks before.

"I'll let you know."

At the end of one sermon, John Wesley asked a plain question for plain people. "Which of you will give yourself soul and body to God?"

David nudged Robert. "That's the question. Are you going to answer?"

Robert shrank back. He liked John Wesley. He liked the way Wesley talked about God. Somehow he knew that Mother was with God. But answer that simple question? No, he couldn't do it.

Chapter Six

THE
SOUND
OF VICTORY

A few days later Robert sat on a stone bridge in the heart of Bristol with his peddler's tray at his side. He dangled his feet over the water and nibbled at a small cold pie he had bought at a nearby market stall. A boy about his own age slumped down beside him. Dirty, his hair matted, his face drawn, the boy did not speak but stared out over the water.

Something prompted Robert to ask, "Are you hungry?"

Without looking directly at him, the boy nodded.

On impulse, Robert shoved the whole pie into the boy's hands. It made him feel good to see how the boy wolfed down the food.

"What's your name?" Robert asked.

"John Woolley. Call me Jack."

Robert noticed Jack's dirty clothes had been neatly mended. Surely Jack must have a mother. "Do you live here?"

Jack nodded.

"Are your parents living?"

Jack kicked his feet against the stone arch of the bridge. "Yes," he said sullenly.

"Why aren't you home — or at school?" Robert sensed that Jack was not an ordinary street boy like those in London who lived off their wits.

Jack shrugged. "I was at school, but — "

"But what?"

"The teacher put me out."

"Why?" Robert was growing more and more curious about Jack. "I should think you'd want to learn everything you could about reading and writing."

Jack turned to him. "Then why aren't you in school?"

"I had to earn my living, but if I had a chance I'd be in school."

Jack scowled and gnawed at his thumbnail. Then Robert caught on. "You've run away," he announced.

"How could you tell?" Jack seemed genuinely surprised. "Anyway, I had to."

"Why?"

"Something's chasing me."

Robert could not help looking around. "Where?"

"It's not anybody you can see." Jack hit his chest with a clenched fist. "It's in here."

Robert stared at him, baffled. If this had been one of the people attending John Wesley's preachings, Robert would have thought Jack was seeking God and did not know it. Was Jack feeling a sense of sin, the way people had to do before they were converted?

"It's the devil after me," Jack blurted.

Robert drew back, startled.

Jack clenched his fists. "He's after me with all his might. He wants me to hang myself or throw myself in the river."

"I know a man who could help you."

"No one can help me."

Robert tried to think how he could be of help. "What will you do, then? You can't stay here. Why don't you go home?"

Jack kicked his heels against the stones even harder than before. "I can't go back."

"You can't live out on the streets for the rest of your life."

"Oh, yes, I can." Jack sprang up and darted away. The last Robert saw of him, Jack slipped into a narrow alley near the river's edge.

Robert stared after him. Why did people run away from help? To run away from home the way Jack had done was a sin. Of course that wasn't the same as grown-ups did, swearing, drinking, beating up one another. *I'm not a sinner. I don't do any of those things*, Robert told himself. "There's another kind of sin," something inside him whispered. But what could it be?

Hadn't Mr. Wesley himself said that as a boy he hoped to be saved by not being as bad as other people? He read his Bible, went to church, said his prayers. *I do that, too*, Robert argued with himself. Why wasn't that being converted?

Father could not answer that question later on. "Something changes inside of you," he said. "Until that happens, you can do all these other things and they will not equal conversion."

David just shook his head when Robert asked, "What is conversion?"

When John Wesley told about going to America to convert the Indians, Robert listened intently. How could a pagan red man know anything about sin?

John Wesley told about an old Indian he had met. "What do you think you are made for?" he asked the man.

"He that is above knows what He made us for," the Indian said. "We know nothing. We are in the dark. But white men know much. And yet white men build great houses as if they were to live forever. But white men cannot live forever. In a little time, white men will be dust as well as I."

John Wesley had replied, "If red men will learn the Good Book, they may know as much as white men. But neither we nor you can understand that Book unless we are taught by Him who is above, and He will not teach you unless you avoid what you already know is not good."

"I believe that," the Indian said. "He will not teach us while our hearts are not right. And our men do what they know is not good: they kill their own children."

After telling this story, John Wesley added, "I have seen some so-called Christians who were worse than the wildest Indians I ever met in America."

To think that even the Indians in America knew there was something in people that told them whether or not they were doing wrong! Robert puzzled over Wesley's statement, "I had a fair weather religion. I could talk well and believe myself, while no danger was near, but in a storm, when death looked me in the face, I asked myself, 'What if the gospel isn't true?'"

Why couldn't people just accept the Bible and its truth? Why did some people object so loudly? When John Wesley preached from the window of an upper room in the house of a gray-headed old silversmith named Dibble, people crowded into the yard and overflowed into the streets.

One man kept saying, "Avoid the false teacher."

In other meetings, people came just to criticize. Sometimes such persons felt God's Spirit whether they wanted to or not. A doctor and a Quaker were two people convinced against their will that God was working through John Wesley.

One day on the street with his peddler's tray, Robert heard a man named John Haydon tell another, "These Methodists fall into strange fits. Come and see for yourself."

"Oh, this has happened before," another man said. "Why, in 1630, at Stewarton, Scotland, converts were affected so much that people called it the 'Stewarton sickness.'"

"See for yourself," John Haydon urged. "I constantly attend public prayers and sacraments, but I'm against Dissenters of every denomination. All these meetings with John Wesley preaching, I call a delusion of the devil."

On the street the next day, Robert heard that John Haydon was raving mad. He had sat down to dinner, a man said, but wanted to finish a sermon he had been reading. At the last page, he suddenly changed color, fell off his chair, screaming and beating himself against the ground.

Several people wanted to see what had happened to John Haydon. Robert followed them to Haydon's house. The place was already full of people.

"Please go away," Mrs. Haydon pleaded.

"No, let them all come," Mr. Haydon shouted. "Let all the world see the just judgment of God."

Two or three men were holding him as quiet as they could. Word had been sent to John Wesley. When he came in, Mr. Haydon burst out, "Yes, this is the man I said deceived the people, but God has overtaken me. I said his teaching is a delusion of the devil, but I was wrong."

John Wesley and others prayed with him. Mr. Haydon found peace in his new faith. "God has put a new song in his mouth," people said. Later, Wesley preached on the text, "Except you are converted, and become as little children, you cannot enter into the kingdom of heaven."

More and more people were overcome by the preaching. Others argued, "Mr. Wesley, don't take people's cries or tears to mean people have given up their sins."

"I have heard these things with my own ears and have seen them with my eyes," John Wesley replied. "I have seen persons changed in a moment from the spirit of fear, horror, and despair to the spirit of love, joy, and peace and to a pure desire of doing the will of God. Tears and crying out are not the fruits. The results are found in how they live afterward. God does forgive sins. If He allows people to become excited and faint, who am I to question His wisdom?"

"Such things are purely natural effects," some sniffed.

"Those people fainted away because of the heat and closeness of the room," others said.

Still others maintained, "It is all a cheat. They could help it if they wanted to."

Wesley kept on preaching, "God is not willing any should perish, but that all should come to repentance." To make room for the societies of Nicholas and Baldwin streets, he bought a piece of ground in the Horsefair near St. James's churchyard. The first stone was laid on May 12, 1739, a date Robert determined to remember.

There was more talk. This time David brought the news. George Whitefield wrote from London that he would have nothing to do with Wesley's new meetinghouse.

That was true, Robert found out, but for a good reason. George Whitefield insisted that John Wesley be responsible for the debt on the building of more than a hundred and fifty pounds.

"I hope this new room of Wesley's means he'll preach inside," someone grumbled later. "This field preaching is indecent."

Wesley admitted field preaching seemed very strange to him at first. "I used to think saving souls was almost a sin if it wasn't done in a church. Now I wonder at those who still talk so loud of the indecency of field preaching. The highest indecency is in St. Paul's Church, when a considerable part of the congregation are asleep, or talking, or looking about, not minding what the preacher says. On the other hand, there is the highest decency in a churchyard or field when the whole congregation behave and look as if they saw the Judge of all and heard Him speaking from heaven."

By this time, John Wesley had a full schedule of preaching appointments in and near Bristol.

"Mr. Wesley is going to preach in Bath next Tuesday," David informed Father one day.

Father needed no further encouragement. "We'll take the wagon and be there."

The city of Bath was shaped like an enormous saucer. Well-dressed people crowded its narrow, winding streets.

"What do people do here?" Robert asked Father.

A traveler, whose vast neckerchief was tied in a bow, and whose dark trousers were stuffed into top boots, overheard Robert's question. "Why, they take the baths, of course," he answered. "They've been here since Roman times, these baths. Then there's cards, gambling, or going to a pub like Horrid Tom's. Of course, if you're an invalid, you go to the King's Bath near the southwest side of the Abbey Church. It's open air, you know."

The traveler volunteered to act as guide. Robert gazed at the green water of the baths and was amazed at seeing ladies with elegant headdresses move slowly through the water pushing floating pans with dainty handkerchiefs, snuffboxes, and flowers.

"Notice that the men at Bath don't wear swords anymore," the volunteer guide remarked. "Beau Nash forbade it."

"Who is Beau Nash?"

"The Master of Ceremonies. He's really the king here. As far back as 1706, he had a night watch installed, arrested vagrants, and had the streets swept. He tells people what to do, and they do it. Yes, sir, Beau Nash is a man I'd never want to cross. He has made his own rules, and they're good rules, too. If he doesn't think a person is good for business, he runs him out of town. Or I should say he *drums* him out."

The volunteer guide's words became clearer the next morning when people assembled outdoors to hear John Wesley preach.

"The great man has heard of John Wesley," a bystander said, "and he does not like him. Everyone knows what that means. John Wesley will be drummed out of town."

A richly dressed lady sniffed to her companion. "I don't know why you insisted I come. It's repulsive, impertinent, disrespectful."

"In what way?"

"Why, the idea of trying to level all ranks and do away with class distinctions! It's monstrous to be told you have a heart as sinful as the common wretches that crawl the earth, and I understand that is what this John Wesley keeps saying. Are you going to listen to such ideas?"

"I think you'll benefit," her companion said. "Maybe you'll even be saved."

"Like my cleaning woman?" the rich lady snorted. "Do you think a woman like that, who says, 'Noo, luv, hoo are you? Hoo's your mother' is *saved*?"

"According to Preacher John Wesley, yes. God's

68

salvation is for everyone."

John Wesley told his hearers, "The Scripture has included all people under sin, high and low, rich and poor alike."

Everyone listened intently. In the distance kettle-drums and French horns sounded.

"It's Beau Nash and his band," people whispered. "He's coming to drum John Wesley out of Bath."

The drumbeats grew louder. Was it the sound of victory for Beau Nash, the ruler of Bath, or was victory going to be in God's hands?

Chapter Seven

THE
INNER WITNESS

All the people who had gathered to hear John Wesley preach outdoors craned their necks to see what Beau Nash would do. Robert stared at the self-proclaimed ruler of Bath. Beau Nash wore a cream-colored three-cornered hat dipped over his right eye. A black wig framed his long, ruddy face. The nostrils of his long, narrow nose quivered, and his small mouth, with its protruding lower lip, turned down in anger. Nash toyed with the lace at his wrists and silenced the three French horns and three kettledrums with a gesture.

Looking down at John Wesley, Beau Nash snapped, "By what authority are you preaching here at Bath?"

"By the authority of Jesus Christ conveyed to

me by the Archbishop of Canterbury when he laid hands upon me and said, 'Take thou authority to preach the gospel.' "

"This is contrary to the Act of Parliament." Beau Nash looked over the crowd. "This is an illegal meeting."

"That's not true," John Wesley said. "It is not contrary to the Act."

"I say it is," Beau Nash announced. "Besides, your preaching frightens people."

John Wesley's listeners murmured protests.

"Sir, did you ever hear me preach?"

Beau Nash drew a fancy handkerchief from his flowered waistcoat and coughed delicately into it. "No."

"How can you judge what you never heard?"

Beau Nash turned down the corners of his mouth in scorn. "By common report."

"Common report is not enough." John Wesley spoke in his usual pleasant voice. "Allow me, sir, to ask if your name is Nash?"

"Yes." Nash stretched upward with a kingly disdain.

"Sir, I dare not judge you by common report. I think it not enough to judge by."

The crowd murmured approval. Robert watched Nash's eyes narrow as if he were about to shift his attack.

"What do the people come here for, Mr. Wesley?"

Before John Wesley could answer, an old woman spoke up. "Let an old woman answer him. You, Mr. Nash, take care of your body. We take care of our souls, and for the good of our souls we come here."

The approving murmur from the crowd swelled like an incoming tide. Nash turned abruptly, motioned to his musicians, and marched away. God became ruler of Bath that day for all who wanted to hear.

On the street later, people thronged to see John Wesley, even though they had no intention of listening to him preach.

"Which one is he?" Robert heard person after person ask.

"I am he," John Wesley kept saying, and the questioners fell silent.

Ten or twelve finely dressed ladies cornered him. Wesley faced them. "I suppose you want to look at me. You're welcome to do so. I don't expect the rich of the world to hear me, I speak plain truth, a thing you know little of, and don't care to know."

For a moment no one replied. Then a lady asked, "Mr. Wesley, do you forbid card playing and dancing?"

People pressed close to listen. Robert was sure he knew the answer. John Wesley's "No, I do not forbid it," surprised him. Hadn't Wesley himself said, "Deliver me from a half Christian"? How could anyone be a Christian who played cards or danced?

"Why don't you forbid it?" someone in the crowd asked in a shocked voice.

"Because it's beginning at the wrong end," John Wesley said.

"But your rules — "

"Rules are for awakened people," Wesley explained. "No man can be bullied into heaven. The grace of God will make the personal application clear. If you take a rattle from a child, he will be angry. Give him something better first, and he will throw the rattle away himself."

"Then can I be saved if I dance or play cards?" a lady insisted.

"Possibly *you* may be saved even though you dance or play cards, but I could not," John Wesley informed her.

"I can't give up my cards."

"You think you can't be happy without them?" Wesley asked.

"No, sir, I could not."

"Then, madam, they are your god. They must save you."

The lady's face turned white, then flushed. She put her hands to her face and turned away.

Robert learned later that she had been converted.

Conversion! That word again. What was the experience like? Robert had to put that question out of his mind during the hours he sold ribbons, laces, and pins to housewives.

At one house a girl and a boy came out, followed by a worried old woman. "Sarah, I don't think you and Peter should go back to the mine this soon, sick as you both were all week.'"

"We'll be all right, Grandmother," Sarah replied.

"Well, here's the day's food for your father and mother." The grandmother thrust a packet into Sarah's hands.

Curious about the mine, Robert followed Sarah and Peter. On the other side of a sloped meadow, he saw a big pile of dirt beside a mine shaft. Sarah sat next to a kind of wheel and frantically tugged at a thick rope. Peter was nowhere in sight.

Sarah glanced over her shoulder. "I — I can't do it." Tears raced down her cheeks. "He's face down in the muck."

"What happened?"

"I couldn't hold the rope, and Peter fell clear to the bottom. See for yourself."

Robert peered down a frightening, narrow shaft. At first all was blackness. Then he saw Peter sprawled head down in the muddy bottom.

"I was just letting him down with the day's food," Sarah said. "He said he could hold on to the rope without making a loop. I shouldn't have let him. It was very foolish. He's just getting over the fever."

It made Robert dizzy just to look into the gaping hole. "Is there any way I could go down and pull him out?"

"Of course," Sarah said. She wound the rope on the windlass. "My father and mother are down there, but they couldn't hear me even if I called."

"Your *mother*?" Robert gasped. "In a mine?"

"Of course. Children are working down there, too." She looped the rope around Robert, after putting his tray in a safe place.

He looked down the shaft. "Are you sure you can hold onto the rope?"

"Oh, yes. The windlass will hold it. The only reason Peter fell was that he didn't make a loop."

"How do we get back up?"

"Oh, I forgot to tell you. Peter will sit on your lap facing you. So go ahead. Just push yourself away from the side and I'll unwind the rope," Sarah instructed.

Robert gulped and tried to be brave. Feeling awkward and trembling a bit, he pushed off from the side of the mine shaft. The rope jerked and he dropped a few feet. Another lurch and darkness enclosed him. He looked up. The sky had never seemed so blue. Tufts of green grass at the lip of the shaft seemed to lean toward him. Why had he never noticed how beautiful grass could be?

Each time the rope jerked, Robert felt the sickening sensation that he was dropping into an endless pit. The floor of the mine rose quicker than he expected, and he found himself sitting in the mud with his knees to his chin. He scrambled up and shook Peter's shoulder.

"Uh — what? What's the matter, Sarah? Is it time to get up?" Peter stared at Robert. "Who are you? What happened?"

Robert explained.

"I'm really all right, just weak, I guess," Peter said.

"Are you ready to go up?"

"Not until I take this food to my mother and father." He called up to Sarah. "I'm all right. We'll be back in a little while." He turned to Robert. "You're going with me, aren't you?"

Peter pointed to a tunnel hardly waist high. "This way. Stoop down if you don't want to bump your head."

Faint candlelight glimmered in the distance. Men moved around on all fours. Women threw chunks of coal into baskets on wheels, and children with ropes

Peter pointed to a tunnel hardly waist-high. "Stoop down if you don't want to bump your head," he said.

around their waists dragged the coal wagons through the tunnels.

Robert was experiencing a whole new set of feelings, mostly in his stomach. The damp earth seemed to move in on him from all sides. How could anyone stay down here for more than a few minutes, let alone days, weeks, months, and years?

Whistling, Peter moved ahead. Robert followed, humped over, cringing at every step. The moist earth stuck to his shoes. He could hardly breathe. How could people work in holes like this for a whole lifetime? No wonder the Kingswood miners were considered to be different from other people. Did God want men to live like moles to earn their daily bread?

A sudden fear engulfed Robert. He couldn't stay down here. He would smother. Already he was gasping for air. He remembered Wesley's fear of storms at sea during his voyage to America, and how a wise man had told Wesley to be still and go on. The thought calmed Robert. After all, the people working in the mine were not gasping for air or clawing at their throats. They just went ahead with their tasks like the Moravian group on board ship who remained utterly calm in the midst of the storm, even women and children.

After Peter delivered the food to his parents, he showed Robert how to hold him on his lap for the trip up. Robert was so relieved to be on top of the ground he could have kissed the grass. He found out that his new Kingswood friends would be going to school in the morning before work. Their parents went, too.

77

"Why don't you go, Robert?"

Robert hedged. "I can already read. I can do arithmetic in my head and make change as fast as my father. So who needs a school?" *What made me say that?* he asked himself. It was the very opposite of what he would like to do.

Maybe that is how people feel before they are converted, he thought afterward. At every preaching he tried to determine beforehand who would be touched by the mysterious experience of conversion. Father always listened with his usual attention, but he already knew what conversion was. David listened, too, his head thrust forward and his gaze fixed on John Wesley

"Maybe we're too young to think about such things," Robert told David.

"Then what about those ten children admitted into one of the bands not long ago?" David asked.

"Why didn't you go to that meeting and stand up with them?" Robert challenged.

David gave him a strange look. "What about yourself?"

"I know Father would like us both to stand up and be counted, and I wish I could, but I can't. I just can't."

"We'll just have to listen some more," David said.

Although hundreds of people listened eagerly to every word John Wesley spoke, some reacted in anger.

Robert overhead one man tell Mr. Wesley, "I like nothing you do. You may preach all you want, but I will never listen to you again."

Others objected as strongly, yet would be overcome by God's power. After their conversion they sang God's praises as loudly as they had denied Him before.

After one of John Wesley's sermons, a large, stocky man with full red cheeks planted himself squarely in front of Wesley and waved a walking stick in front of his nose. "Mr. Wesley, I object to your manner of preaching."

John Wesley replied in his usual quiet but plain way. "I have no more right to object to a man for holding a different opinion from mine than I have to differ from a man because he wears a wig and I wear my own hair."

"The field preaching you do is hardly suitable for a gentleman," the man continued.

"The devil does not like field preaching," John Wesley remarked. "Neither do I. I love a comfortable room, a soft cushion, and a handsome pulpit, but you may remember our Lord's Sermon on the Mount was the earliest example of field preaching."

The stocky man glared and continued criticizing. "You do not have a parish of your own."

"And I probably never shall have one," John Wesley replied. "There are many churches which will not permit me to declare the mighty works of God."

"Exactly my point, sir. Exactly my point," the man said in triumph. "How is it, then, that you lure Christians away from the Church of England which you claim to be your church, too? Why do you assemble these innocent people to pray, hear Scripture, and sing songs that you and your brother have written and published as hymnbooks?" The man jabbed his walking stick into the ground several times for emphasis. "How do you justify these actions, sir?"

"I do not think it hard to justify what I do," Wesley said. "Permit me to speak plainly. God in Scripture commands me, according to my power, to instruct the ignorant, reform the wicked, and confirm the virtuous. Whom shall I hear? Man or God?"

By this time several people had gathered around to listen. Robert, Father, and David stood with them.

"You speak very plain, sir. Is this why you call yourself a Christian?"

"I am not a Christian," Wesley said quietly.

Several people gasped.

"But you could not preach as you do if you were not a Christian," a woman exclaimed.

The stocky man rested both hands on his walking stick. "What do you mean by saying you are not a Christian?"

"I only follow Christ," Wesley replied.

The man continued to attack Wesley with words. "Why do you carry on as you do?"

"Because I desire to be a Christian. I must live by my convictions. On this principle I went to America and to the Moravians in Germany. On the same principle, I am ready at any time, with God as my helper, to go to Abyssinia or China, wherever it pleases God to call me. I look upon all the world as my parish."

The stocky man's red cheeks grew redder still. He muttered angrily under his breath, and with a final flourish of his walking cane stomped off. Later, he too was converted.

Why does God work this way? Robert asked himself. Why couldn't people just open up to God like the grain ripening in the field? Hadn't Wesley preached about the kingdom of God as being like growing grain? A man planted a seed and watched it spring up in a mysterious way, first the blade, then the ear, then the full corn in the ear.

But what about the rainstorm that beat down the grain? Afterward, if it survived, it grew all the stronger. John Wesley endured storms, the storms of men's wrath turned toward him. But he had an answer. "The more evil that men say of me for my Lord's sake, the more good He will do for me." He told how his own father had said the strongest proof of Christianity was the inner witness.

Robert puzzled over these ideas. What was God's secret? Was it His plan to test man's endurance? Endurance of what? *Sin,* Robert decided. But what was the greatest sin? His own inner witness spoke up. Man's greatest sin was deliberately preventing God's loving plan for salvation.

Is that my sin? Am I denying God? On that point, Robert's inner witness remained silent.

THE
FOUNDRY

People all over the countryside were being led by John Wesley into a new relationship with God. His preaching had reached thousands. Now came news of backsliding in London at Fetter Lane among the very people who had accepted Christ in their lives. Robert puzzled over this mystery. How could people turn their backs on what had given them new life? What would John Wesley do?

"I have received another pressing letter from London," Wesley told his listeners one day. "Our brethren in Fetter Lane need me and I must go."

"But surely God still has a work for you to do here in Bristol," his listeners protested. "What about your brother Charles? Can't he take care of this problem?"

But John Wesley felt he had to return to London. His brother Charles was not an organizer. He preferred to praise God with the hymns which he wrote by the dozen. "In one sense I am the head and Brother Charles is the heart of this work," Wesley explained.

"But where will this all lead?" someone asked.

John Wesley had an answer. "I am not concerned about what may be a hundred years hence. He who governed the world before I was born will take care of it likewise when I am dead. My part is to improve the present moment."

To improve the present moment meant using a method, Robert found out. John Wesley chose leaders to be in charge of the Methodist groups in Bristol. Each group followed the same plan of worship, including the singing of hymns written by Charles Wesley.

On the day John Wesley left for London, Father asked Robert and David, "Are you boys ready to go back to London, too?"

"Yes," they chorused.

David's eyes gleamed with what seemed to Robert to be a hidden purpose. In London he found out what was on David's mind — his Uncle Jem, in prison.

"Have you been worrying about him all this time?"

"Yes, and praying for him, too."

"Let's go see him."

David brightened. "Could we?"

While Father went off to pay for his peddler's wagon and buy more supplies, Robert and David went to the huge stone prison. At the entrance, the turnkey, a slender man with a white face and long red nose, asked what they wanted.

"I've come to see my uncle," David said.

The turnkey fingered a big metal ring with at least twenty keys dangling from it' "Who is your uncle?"

"Jem Elliott."

The turnkey started to say something but checked himself. A woman with a small boy came in and asked to see her husband. "It's all a mistake that he's here."

"They all say that," the turnkey grunted. "Come along, all of you." He led the way down a dark hall. Cells with thick black bars lined each side. The stench of human beings living in their own filth choked Robert. He remembered the coal tunnels at Kingswood. What was the difference between the miners and these prisoners? Criminals could stand straight up in their cells, but hardworking miners had to stoop. How strange life could be!

The turnkey stopped at a cell and gestured with his thumb. "Your husband is in there. Do you have a little something for my trouble?"

"Something? Oh." The woman dug into a cloth pouch and handed the turnkey a coin. Someone called to him and he hurried off.

The little boy peered into his father's cell. "Father, why are you staying in there? Why does that man have such big keys? Is that board your bed? Why don't you put some clean straw on the floor?" The boy clung to the barred door with both hands. "What a funny kind of door this is."

The woman explained to her husband that she would be going to the workhouse.

"Which one?" her husband asked.

"St. Thomas's. I can spin wool and flax, or sew or knit, or wind silk and earn money," the woman said. "They'll teach our boy to read and write. We'll get along fine. Don't worry."

"I must tell you something. It's today," the husband said.

The woman bowed her head in silent weeping.

"Don't weep. "I'm going to meet my Savior today."

The woman raised her head. Her cheeks flushed in sudden joy.

"Yes, all your prayers have been answered. The Methodists came, and then there's a man here who has helped, too — Jem Elliott. We'll both be victorious in just a little while."

David tugged at Robert's sleeve. "Let's not wait for the turnkey. We can find Uncle Jem ourselves."

Robert and David looked into every cell. Some prisoners lay on the floor asleep. Others groaned or cursed. An old officer in uniform fingered his watch and chain. "I'll send these to the pawn-broker's," Robert heard him mutter.

The turnkey came and showed the boys Uncle Jem's cell. "I don't understand what has happened to him," the turnkey said. "Never saw such goings-on in my life. A man about to be hanged — " He broke off sharply.

David did not seem to hear. "Uncle Jem?" he called into the cell.

"What, lad? Is it you? Have you come to see me on this glorious day of all days?" Uncle Jem thrust both hands between the bars and pumped David's hand.

"What is happening today?" David asked.

"What a blessed morning this is," Uncle Jem went on. "Oh, when will the hour come when my soul shall be set at liberty?"

"What is it, Uncle Jem? What are you talking about?"

"Lad, when I came here, my heart was as hard as the walls of my cell, but not anymore. Oh, if I could only tell the thousandth part of the joys I feel."

Robert saw David struggle to understand. "Uncle Jem, did the Methodists come?"

Uncle Jem beamed. "God sent them to me. God has forgiven my sins, and I am ready to meet my Maker today."

"Are you sure it is today?" David faltered.

"Yes, indeed. The bellman came just after midnight and said the most welcome words, 'Remember, you are to die today,' and I said, 'Welcome news.' Do not weep for me, David. I am going home."

In saying good-bye, David managed a smile. Outside the prison walls crowds had already gathered to wait for the death carts to take the doomed prisoners away to be hanged.

David lingered, staring at the wooden sides of the death carts.

"Come away," Robert urged.

David remained silent most of the way home. "If God has forgiven Uncle Jem, why can't people forgive him, too?" he burst out.

"I guess it's not enough to say you're sorry. You have to pay for what you've done."

"But what good does that do when — when you're dead?"

"David, the soul doesn't die." The strength of his own belief surprised Robert. But hadn't John Wesley told him about the soul the first time they met?

In the next few months the pattern of John Wesley's ministry became clearer. By preaching, printing booklets of sermons, and talking to people Wesley brought the Word of God into the lives of seekers as no one man had ever done before in England.

"How can he remember everything?" Robert asked himself. He knew the Bible. He knew Latin. Robert had overheard John Wesley and his brother Charles talking together *in Latin*. They did it every day. Wesley knew Greek, too.

Robert saw John Wesley mount a horse one rainy day. Wesley opened his umbrella to its amazing five-foot spread, clapped his spectacles on his near-sighted eyes, and took out his Greek Testament, smaller than his outstretched hand. He jogged off to a meeting, reading on the way.

How could a person learn so much? Of course, John Wesley had gone to Charterhouse School when he was only six, and kept on going to school until he had finished college at Oxford.

I could never do that. It's too late for me even to think about it, Robert told himself. Just going to school was not the answer to all that John Wesley accomplished. Being converted was not the answer either. After conversion a person had to spend his time doing good both for himself and others, but John Wesley did something more. He kept both a diary and a journal accounting for how he spent his time every hour of the day.

By preaching, printing booklets, and talking to people Wesley brought the Word of God to seekers all over England.

"How does he find the time to write so much?" Robert asked Father.

"He writes in shorthand," Father said.

"That's like learning Latin and Greek," Robert exclaimed. Why did he even think about it? It was enough to earn a living by peddling and to hear John Wesley preach between trips to Bristol. People there had begun to quarrel almost as soon as Wesley left for London the first time. Wherever he himself went, he brought peace. *What good was all that Latin and Greek?* Robert asked himself. *Why do I even ask? These things don't concern me.*

Some things did concern him, like John Wesley's buying the old foundry. It stood on Windmill Hill, next to Moorfields, a city park with trees and grass. At the northwest corner the Lord Mayor had a doghouse where the city hounds were kept. Close by was a tollgate, called the Dog-Bar. The whole area would be interesting to explore.

"Let's go see the foundry," Robert suggested.

"Not me," David said with such vehemence Robert stared in surprise. "That's where they store ammunition. I wouldn't go in there for any amount of money you'd give me."

"Why not? Mr. Wesley bought it so there would be enough room for everybody. When he gets it fixed up, there will be one room that can hold fifteen hundred people. So come on. Let's go look at it."

David did not budge. "That's where they store ammunition, I told you. One time a piece of it blew up and killed a whole lot of people. Do you want to go there and get yourself blown up?"

"That was more than twenty years ago," Robert

told David later. "They were going to melt down a French cannon and recast it. People came to watch. A man warned everyone to leave because there would be danger of an explosion when the hot metal was poured. Not everyone left, and the rest were hurt when part of the roof blew out. There isn't any ammunition in there now."

David agreed to look at the deserted foundry, with its coach house and stable in back, its ceiling showing broken plaster, and its walls upheld by rotting beams. "How can they ever fix it up?" he asked.

Robert shared his dismay. What a place for John Wesley to preach in! Not only that, but John Wesley was going to live at the foundry, and his mother was going to live there, too.

Wesley preached in the foundry even before the repairs were finished. His pulpit, made of rough planks nailed together, was not the handsome kind Wesley once smilingly admitted he would enjoy. At his first service on a Sunday evening at five o'clock, Wesley preached to hundreds of people. As usual, the women sat apart from the men, on benches instead of pews.

John Wesley did more than preach at the foundry.

"Did you hear about the charity school Mr. Wesley is starting?" David asked Robert in excitement.

"Charity school? Who wants to go to a charity school like poor people?" Robert retorted.

"*I* do, and I'm going."

"Well, I'm not. I know all I need to know." Why had he spoken so strongly? Robert wondered. Now he could never back down. He learned that the school was held from six in the morning until noon, and again from one until five. He heard that the teacher, Silas Todd, gave up a position as clerk to teach for ten shillings a week.

Children in rags came to the school. The Methodist women sewed for them. "No Methodist should ever be in rags," Wesley said.

Robert earned enough money to buy the clothes he needed. "No charity for me," he told himself.

"Why don't you go to school with David?" his father kept asking.

"I'd rather earn my living."

"Mr. Wesley says Silas Todd is an understanding man," Father said.

Robert had heard that, too, and also that Mr. Wesley had added, "but not very educated." That remark convinced Robert even more not to go. Robert wanted only the best education or none at all.

What was it John Wesley said once? "If anyone will convince me of my errors I will heartily thank him."

If I'm wrong, someone will have to convince me, Robert told himself.

Chapter Nine

MOTHER
OF
METHODISM

R obert stood with a group of people in front of the foundry and waited for the coach to bring John Wesley's mother to live with him. Two old men chatted near him.

"It's a strange thing."

"A strange thing indeed."

"He came back from America a failure. He said so himself."

"Yes, and his brother Charles, too."

The first man shaded his eyes from the sun and looked down the road. "Not in sight," he announced. "I heard that Mr. Wesley's mother had many a word to say about his going to America."

"Indeed, she has said many a word these many years," the second man chuckled.

"Yes, but for a woman, they say she speaks right good sense."

"She should have persuaded her sons to stay in England where they belonged. It was a mistake to try to convert Indians. They are savages. Oxford men should not have busied themselves in such affairs."

A third man joined the group. "I knew them. I knew the Wesleys well up there in Epworth. These brothers are not a bit like their father, old Samuel Wesley. He was a preacher, too, and mighty strict. Well do I remember back in 1705 standing on the cold floor of his church in my bare feet Sunday after Sunday."

"Why did you have to do that?" someone asked.

"Some little sin or other. Mostly because I spoke up, out of turn, you might say."

A woman remarked, "I understand the Wesley children didn't get along with the other children there in Epworth."

The man from Epworth agreed. "I remember my own parents shouting at them, 'Be off with you, you devil's brats. We'll soon have you out begging.' Nineteen children Mrs. Wesley bore, and those that didn't die, she taught herself in the kitchen of the parsonage."

What would it be like to have a mother around all the time? Robert choked with sudden feeling. Maybe if his mother had lived, things would be different. Maybe he could even go to a charity school without loss of pride.

He listened to the man from Epworth tell about old Samuel Wesley's poetry. "He called himself the

'Island Poet of Axholme,' even if the island was only a bit of old England surrounded by rivers and canals."

"How did he get the church at Epworth?"

"For a poem he'd written for the Queen. He got fifty pounds a year for it, but that didn't keep him out of prison for debt. I remember he owed three hundred pounds, and this Mr. Pinder wanted his money back in one hour. Imagine that! Old Mr. Wesley had used the money just to keep his family going, and he couldn't raise the money in an hour. He would have to sell his furniture and livestock. Well, this Mr. Pinder was going to agree, but some Dissenters said Mr. Wesley ought to be put in prison, so they took him to Lincoln and put him in a debtors' prison there."

A murmur from the onlookers stopped the Epworth man's story. A coach with four horses lumbered into view.

"It's John Wesley's mother! She's here!"

Everyone crowded around the coach. A tiny, pale woman with a hooked nose and bright eyes waved through the little window. She leaned back on the seat and closed her eyes.

"Isn't she coming out?" a woman asked.

"She's been ill, they say. Has to be carried."

John Wesley came around, opened the coach door, and reached in to help his mother. Susannah Wesley put her hand into his and with a firm step descended from the coach. With a glance as firm as her step, she surveyed the curious onlookers. Robert felt the power of her glance.

"So these are the Methodists," Susannah Wesley said.

"And you are the mother," someone ventured.

Susannah Wesley acknowledged the tribute with a nod and a half smile.

"Sick or not, she's a spunky little woman," Robert heard someone say in a low voice.

Mrs. Wesley took command of unloading her boxes. Robert helped carry them upstairs to the apartment. Afterward, he lingered behind, strangely drawn to this little woman, the mother of Methodism.

"Is there anything else I can do for you, Mrs. Wesley?"

Susannah Wesley leaned back in a winged chair and folded her hands. "Sit down." She gestured toward an odd-shaped chair with a drawer in the bottom and a flat board backrest. "There, in the drop-leaf chair, or over there in the study chair."

The study chair had a most peculiar shape, with a curved black leather arm at the top and a book-board above that. But how could a person sit in the chair and read a book? The backrest was so narrow a person could not sit comfortably.

Embarrassed, Robert chose the drop-leaf chair. He could not imagine why a chair would be made in this way.

Mrs. Wesley watched him with a slight smile. "What is your name?"

"Robert Upton."

"Why aren't you in the school my son has started?"

"I have to learn — I mean I have to earn my living." Robert felt his cheeks flush. Why had he made such a stupid mistake as to say *learn* for earn?

"What do you do for a living, Robert?"

95

Robert described his peddler's tray. "That's how I met Mr. Wesley." He rushed on, telling how he, his father, and David had kept up with John Wesley's preaching schedule in and around Bristol, yet earned their living all the time. "David is in school," he finished. "But I can't go."

"Did anyone say you couldn't go to school?" Mrs. Wesley's question was soft.

"No, but — " How could he explain? Everything seemed so mixed up all of a sudden. Something inside of him kept telling him not to go to school. Whatever it was told him not to worry about being converted. He had enough to do earning his living.

"Are you doing what God wants you to do?"

The question caught Robert unprepared. Wasn't that what he was doing — listening to his inner voice. It was strange, though, how going to school and being converted had anything to do with each other. "Yes. I mean no. I mean I don't know," he babbled.

Susannah Wesley smiled. "I think it will be either the chair you're sitting on or the other one, whichever is most comfortable."

Robert bounced to the edge of the chair. What was she talking about?

"Robert, I haven't been very well, and I'll need someone like you to run errands for me. My sons John and Charles are too busy with their own work to be with me for very long at a time. Do you think you could come by once in a while?"

"Oh, yes. I would like to do that, Mrs. Wesley. But what about the chairs?"

Susannah Wesley smiled, a secret, almost

mischievous smile, Robert thought. What was the mystery of those chairs?

He found out soon enough. One day she handed him a book.

"My eyes are getting so dim. Read me this passage, a favorite of mine."

One glance was enough for Robert. He had never seen such squiggles in his life. "I can't read that. I don't even know what the letters are."

"My children could read their Greek letters by the time they were eight years old." Mrs. Wesley handed Robert paper and a quill pen. "We might as well start today."

"Start — start what?"

"Your education. A quick, bright boy like you should not spend his life peddling." She raised a hand to stop his protests. "Peddling is certainly an honorable work, but I keep feeling that God has something else in mind for you." She gestured to the two mysterious chairs. "Take your choice. Try the drop-leaf one first." She lowered the drop leaf and it became a writing desk. "You sit on this stool facing the chair," she explained.

Robert tried it, but the stool was too low for comfort.

"Try the other one."

"How do you sit in it?"

Susannah Wesley smiled, "Sit astraddle."

So that was the mystery. Robert sat facing the back of the chair. The ledge above the black leather armrest could be used to hold a book or to write on. The chair fit him perfectly.

"My son John studied this way for many an

hour," Mrs. Wesley said. "He preferred the drop-leaf chair, however. He is not as large as you — never weighed more than a hundred and twenty-six pounds, after he was grown."

What would it be like to be part of such a big family? Mrs. Wesley described the schoolroom near the kitchen at the rectory in Epworth.

"When did they start school?"

"They had no lessons until the fifth year," Mrs. Wesley said. "The first day they had to learn the alphabet. The second day, the Bible was brought out and they spelled through the first verse."

Robert tried to imagine such fast learning. "How could they learn so fast?"

"All my children learned the alphabet in one day — all except one," Mrs. Wesley added in a low voice. "They reviewed all they had learned during the morning, and then, before evening prayers they reviewed the afternoon lessons."

Robert gulped. Did Mrs. Wesley expect him to learn the Greek alphabet in one day? He wasn't even sure about the English alphabet. What came after Q, for example? As for the T's and V's, they were simply a buzz in his mind. Why had he bragged to Peter and Sarah back there in Bristol that he could read? Just talking to Mrs. Wesley showed him he knew next to nothing.

Mrs. Wesley's patience with him reached his heart. She told him the same thing again and again until it became part of himself. Before he knew quite what had happened, he was sitting astride the study chair studying the lessons in Greek and Latin Mrs. Wesley assigned him, and continuing most of the day.

"How can you be so patient with me?" he asked one day.

Mrs. Wesley had a faraway look in her eyes. "I remember my husband saying to me, 'You've told that child the same thing twenty times.' I told him, 'If I had mentioned the matter only nineteen times, my efforts would have failed. It was the twentieth time that brought success.'"

She told Robert how she had taught the children to cry softly after the first year. If they gave each other presents, they could not take them back. They called each other 'Brother Samuel,' 'Sister Sukey,' and so on.

"Were they ever bad?" Robert asked.

"They weren't punished if they confessed," Susannah Wesley said. "At the table, they had to eat what was offered and not reach for food. They had to wait for more or whisper to the maid who asked me."

From Mrs. Wesley's stories about life at Epworth, Robert could almost feel what it was like to live with so many brothers and sisters.

"Will you go into the other room and bring whatever coins you find from Mr. Wesley's desk?" Susannah Wesley asked Robert one day.

Robert found the desk, with its twin mirrors, standing open. He saw notes and letters neatly stacked into a half-dozen desk pigeonholes. Where should he look first? He couldn't paw through all these papers. There must be some mistake about money being in this desk.

"I couldn't find any money," he apologized to Mrs. Wesley.

She pressed her hand to her forehead. "I forgot. It's in the secret drawer."

Robert went back, but he could not find anything that looked like a secret drawer. "There isn't any such drawer, Mrs. Wesley," he reported. "Everything is out in the open."

"Pull out the drawer on the right-hand side," she instructed. "Pull it all the way out, and you'll find it."

Robert went back and pulled out the drawer. Nothing there. Really embarrassed now, he reported to Mrs. Wesley.

"When the drawer is clear out, reach in at the side and you'll find a long piece of wood that's loose. Pull it out and on the end you'll see the secret drawer."

Robert slid the wooden slat out. At the end was attached the secret drawer, hardly longer than his hand. He brought back the coins.

"You found it," Mrs. Wesley said. "Good. Now I can pay the postman. Ah, mailing letters is expensive, but it's worth it to keep people in touch."

Several of Mrs. Wesley's daughters lived not too far away. Robert knew Mrs. Wesley grieved about her son Samuel's death the previous November, but she accepted God's will both in her personal life and the life of the Methodists. Her sons were going out to preach more often and farther away.

"Who's in charge of the bands now that John and Charles Wesley are so often on the road?" Robert heard one of the Methodists ask another.

"Thomas Maxfield."

"But he's a layman, isn't he?" the other man asked.

"Yes, but does that matter? He's converted."

"What does he do in the meetings?"

"He reads the Scriptures and explains them. That's all."

But word spread that Thomas Maxfield, a layman, was preaching.

"He is inspired," some said.

Others sniffed. "Kitchen preaching."

Robert asked Mrs. Wesley what *kitchen preaching* meant. Maybe it was something like the kitchen teaching she had done so many years ago.

"When my husband was away, I had meetings in my kitchen," she told Robert. "So many people came they filled the yard clear to the gate."

Robert heard others complain, "She'd better not let any kitchen preaching start here. Neither John nor Charles Wesley would like it."

As everyone soon learned, the Wesley brothers did not like to have a layman preach, but their mother took matters into her own hands.

"Thomas Maxfield has turned preacher, I find," Robert heard John Wesley tell his mother on his return from a preaching trip. The little man was as annoyed as he ever permitted himself to be.

"John," his mother said firmly, "you know what my feelings have been. You cannot suspect me of favoring readily anything of this kind. But be careful how you treat that young man, for he is as surely called of God to preach as you are. Examine the fruits of his preaching, and hear him yourself."

John Wesley was fair. He listened to Thomas Maxfield preach. "It is the Lord's doing," he said. "Let Thomas Maxfield do what seems to him good. Who am I that I should withstand God?"

Robert saw that Mrs. Wesley's sons still listened to her advice.

To think she has time to help me, he thought. What had she said? "You must not pass through the world like straw upon a river," she had told him.

Why had she said that? He was studying hard. Was there something more he had to do?

THE
ENEMY WITHIN

Methodists had enemies. Robert could see that. For every hundred who heard John or Charles Wesley preach, a dozen could be counted on to criticize them or their method.

"Why does everyone praise them so much?" a man asked. "I have a relative who was with them at Oxford when the Holy Club started."

"What's his name?"

"Benjamin Ingham from Yorkshire. He went to America with them and to the Moravians in Germany, too. Indeed, I hear he became a Moravian."

"It seems as if people break away from the Wesleys after a time," someone remarked.

"It's not that," another objected. "They break away from God."

"There must be more than one way to worship God," a third remarked. "The Moravians say to be still and the Methodists say to get busy doing good."

The man's remark was enough to start Robert thinking again. Who could be called Christian? Mrs. Wesley helped.

"If you give God the praise for any well-spent day, you are acting like a Christian. I often hear loud complaints of sin, but rarely, very rarely, any work of prayer and thanksgiving to our dear Lord." She added, "A Christian should live in the world like a stranger in an inn. Use what is necessary, enjoy what he can, but remember that it's not his home."

Some people complained because the Wesley family had Dissenters on both sides.

"I am sorry you turned Dissenter from the Church of England," a man told John Wesley.

"If that is so, I do not know it," Wesley replied. "Our twentieth article defines a true church as 'a congregation of faithful people, wherein the true Word of God is preached and the sacraments duly administered.' The Church of England is that body of faithful people. I belong to it, and always shall."

"But you do not go to the Church of England."

"Indeed I do, and I do not preach except at times when there is no preaching in the church." He continued, "Who are the worst Dissenters from this church? Sabbath-breakers, drunkards, fighters, liars, lovers of money or dress or praise or pleasure more than lovers of God. All these are Dissenters who belong to the synagogue of Satan."

The law of England acknowledged people who

did not agree with the Church of England and called them Dissenters. The people who disagreed with John Wesley had no such name. On a trip to Bristol with Father, Robert saw dozens of people in the two alleys by the New Room in the Horsefair. These people had not come to listen to Wesley preach. They shouted, cursed, and pushed each other toward the door of the New Room.

"Down with the enemy of the church," a man shouted.

"Down with the preacher of false doctrine," called another.

"Out! Out with John Wesley."

The mayor of Bristol, Stephen Clutterbuck, sent orders for the mob to break up. No one moved. The shouts increased. "John Wesley must go!"

The chief constable came in person and tried to quiet the people. The leader stormed, "This is none of your business. Leave him to us. We'll take care of this John Wesley and all of his Methodists."

The chief constable, with several officers of the law, took the ringleaders to court. Mayor Clutterbuck cut their protests off. "What Mr. Wesley does is not for you to decide. I'll keep the peace. I will allow no rioting in this city."

Why did people — more people than ever — hate a man who was trying to show them God's plan for their salvation?

"They're afraid," Father told Robert. Father was studying the Bible every spare minute so that he could become a lay preacher like Thomas Maxfield and others.

Afraid. Why should anyone be afraid? Were they

afraid something would happen to them as it did to John Haydon, who was deathly sick until he confessed his sins and made peace with God?

"Does everyone have to be sick before they're converted?" Robert asked Father.

"No," Father answered. "It is true that Charles Wesley was sick just before his conversion, but John Wesley did not have such a struggle. He felt his heart strangely warmed."

"Then a person doesn't have to be sick to be converted?" Robert did not mean his words to be a question. They were a statement. He remembered John Wesley telling of his early search for the faith which no one can have without knowing he had it.

"Why is it that the Methodists have more and more enemies?" Robert asked Father.

"Because they have more faith."

"But — "

"God tests us by opposites," Father explained. "Faith isn't real faith until it is tried."

"You mean you have to keep this faith no matter what happens?"

"Yes." Father told how John Wesley tried to visit a soldier about to be executed for desertion, and who had been converted. The commanding officer would not let Mr. Wesley or any of his people in because he thought the Methodists were atheists.

The Methodists were called other names, too, such as enthusiasts. "It's just ugly enthusiasm," people would say if converts shouted with the joy of letting Christ live in them. Such joy made enemies. Why?

Robert could only watch and wait for an answer. He knew one thing to be true — John Wesley's statement that it was an "absolute impossibility to be a Christian." Nor could a Christian be, as Wesley put it, "namby-pamby."

Was it so bad to be enthusiastic? Robert remembered Wesley telling about a young man who had asked his opinion about Whitefield's journals. They are enthusiasm from beginning to end," the young man had said. "He talks so much about joy and stuff, and inward feelings. I declare, I cannot tell what to make of it." Wesley told the young man that the inward workings of the Spirit of God might be misunderstood by those who had not felt them.

The young man's comments didn't upset Wesley too much. He was used to criticism. What really hurt him was discovering his misplaced trust in two young men. Gwillam Snowde and Robert Ramsey, whom he hired to teach at the Kingswood School, left after three or four months.

"They took more than thirty pounds of the money collected for building the school," someone exclaimed.

"John Wesley is just too trusting," a man declared.

"But God is with him," another said. "Did you hear what happened to one of the leaders in the riot the other night? He hanged himself. Another one had severe pain for many days, and still another came to Mr. Wesley and said he had become drunk on purpose to stir up the riot, but when he came to the New Room, he could not open his mouth."

"Nothing will prevent God's Word from spreading over England," Father declared. "It's like seed dropped on good soil. Birds may eat some of the seeds. Some may not receive enough water and die, but nobody on earth can destroy all the seeds."

"If storms don't destroy them, the grain grows stronger than before," Robert said. Hadn't he thought something like this before? He was beginning to sound like a preacher himself. *But's that impossible,* he thought. *I don't even want to be a preacher.*

But he watched and listened and waited. Where would John Wesley's preaching lead to next?

Back in London, Robert found out. He heard Charles Wesley declare in his usual abrupt way, "Nine out of ten of you are swallowed up in the dead sea of stillness."

John Wesley told the Fetter Lane members that they had strayed from the faith. They rebelled, for the most part, and did not accept Wesley's statement.

One man had his own idea about being saved. "God knows before they are born which people will love Him. They will be saved, and the others will never be," he told Wesley. "And many of your society believe this, too."

"I never asked whether they think that way or not. Only that they do not trouble others by arguing about it."

"But I will dispute about it."

"Whenever you come?" John Wesley asked.

"Yes."

"Why would you come among us who you know think differently than you?"

"Because you are all wrong," the man said, "and I am resolved to set you all right."

John Wesley advised him not to come.

"Then I will go and tell all the world that you and your brother are false prophets."

Later, at the foundry, Robert heard John Wesley discuss the problem with his mother.

"There is no time to delay. If we do, we shall utterly destroy the cause of God. I must strike at the root of the grand delusion."

At an early morning meeting at the foundry, Wesley fasted, put on his black robe, and with a prayer on his lips he told his people that it was not enough to believe. " 'If you love me, keep my commandments,' " Wesley preached.

To no one's surprise, the Fetter Lane Society broke up. Those who chose to follow John Wesley met after that at the foundry. More and more people joined the Methodists. They still belonged to the Church of England, but they liked being shown a method of fulfilling God's will. John Wesley showed them how. He and his members helped poor people, prisoners, the sick, and the orphans.

"If we see God in all things and do all for Him, then all things are easy," Wesley said. " 'Give to the poor, and you shall have treasure in heaven,' " he often quoted.

How could anyone be offended by John Wesley's preaching? Why were there enemies? Why did some people come to be entertained, as if John Wesley were an actor?

"Come and hear the preaching man. He preaches without a book." Robert heard someone say.

"You mean the Methodist?"

"Yes. It's better than a sideshow on market day."

Yet John Wesley made few gestures when he preached. "Yes, I often speak loud. I often speak vehemently," he admitted, "but I never scream. I never strain myself. I dare not. I know it would be a sin against God."

Wesley never talked long. An ordinary sermon took twenty minutes. "My brother Charles and I both like to speak blunt and plain, without going a great deal round about," he said. He could be blunt about other men's preaching. "I am sick and tired of hearing some men preach Christ. Let some pert, self-sufficient animal who has neither sense nor grace bawl out something about Christ or His blood, and his hearers cry out, 'What a fine gospel sermon.'"

No, John Wesley could not be said to be namby-pamby in his convictions, Robert decided. Maybe that was why he made enemies.

"Never turn your back on a friend or a foe," Wesley said. Sometimes he did not answer a taunt, Robert remembered with amusement. A Dissenter had called out, "*Quid est tibi nomen?*"

"That means 'What is your name?'" Robert whispered to his father. "It's Latin." He explained that John Wesley often talked with his brother in Latin.

Wesley did not answer the man who heckled him.

"See?" the Dissenter told his companions in triumph. "I told you he did not understand Latin."

Other attacks were farfetched.

"I know for a fact that John Wesley keeps two Catholic priests in his house. He gets a large sum of money from Spain, and as soon as the Spaniards land in England, he'll join them with twenty thousand men," a man said.

"Yes, he is a Jesuit. That's plain," another agreed.

Wesley ignored such remarks. He had learned in America that people blamed him for words he never said and actions he never did. He considered his work in America a failure, but he was not going to fail in England.

Which was worse, the enemy within or the enemy without? Robert wondered. Some of John Wesley's friends did not agree with him anymore. George Whitefield, who had once begged Wesley to come to Bristol, had turned Calvinist.

"The Methodists are splitting into two camps," Father said.

What if everyone found God and followed Him without being with other people? Other people made all the trouble.

John Wesley answered that. "Years ago I met a man who told me, 'You cannot serve Him alone. You must therefore find companions or make them. The Bible knows nothing of religion by oneself.'"

People could work together or against each other. Some enemies were outside and some were inside. Thoughts themselves could become enemies. When John Wesley asked after a sermon, "Does anyone feel different? Will you speak of it?" a number of people always responded.

"Then why can't I?" Robert asked himself. Was it because of the enemy within?

111

THE
TEST

A few months later in Bristol on his way to a
meeting at the New Room, Robert saw a boy lurking
in a nearby alley.

"Aren't you Jack Woolley?"

Taller now than when Robert first saw him, Jack's
face showed even more strain than before. "Who
are you?" he asked, edging away.

Robert reminded him of how they had met. "But
you ran away. I knew the man who could help
you — and now here you are. Are you going in?"

"I don't know. I can't make up my mind." Jack's
mouth twisted in pain from his inner struggle.

"Are you sick?"

"No."

"Are you still running away from home?"

112

"Sometimes." Jack kicked at a stone.

"Is the devil still tempting you?"

Jack choked back a sob. "More than before. I don't know what to do. I can't stand it much longer."

Robert grabbed Jack's arm. "You're coming with me. Now."

That night John Wesley spoke of disobedience to parents. Jack listened as if stunned.

"There never in the world was a boy as wicked as I am," he told Robert afterward. "God will never forgive me."

"Of course He will. That's His plan, to save everyone," Robert said.

"Even me?"

"Yes. But there's one thing you have to do first."

"What's that?" Jack asked.

"You have to ask."

Jack hurried off without a word. Robert stared after him. What was Jack going to do? Throw himself into the river? Robert waited for news, but for several days heard nothing. He found out who Jack's mother was and tried to overhear snatches of her talk to others.

"How Jack has changed," Robert heard Mrs. Woolley say one night. "He helps in every way he can. On preaching nights, he feeds the other children their supper and puts them to bed. Oh, he's a blessing in every way." She told how he prayed for his brothers and sisters, for John and Charles Wesley, and for the ministers who were now working with the Wesley brothers in spreading the news of salvation over the country.

The change in Jack Woolley delighted yet puzzled

113

Robert. Here was a boy his own age who had experienced conversion. What was it like?

One day he met Jack, whose face was as bright as if a thousand candles had lit it.

"What happened to you, Jack?"

"I was wrestling against the devil and praying God to deliver me. Suddenly, I was in the midst of a light so filled with joy that I hardly knew where I was. Oh, it's hard to explain, but I love all mankind so much I could lie on the ground for my worst enemies to trample on."

Robert could understand struggling and wrestling in prayer. Many Methodists had described that experience. He understood how a person could have peace inside even when being tested by enemies. John and Charles Wesley were examples, although Charles had a quick temper. But how could love of God and mankind make a person want to have his enemies trample on him?

Then Jack became ill. When Robert visited him, Jack announced, "I shall die, but do not cry for me. What a joyful thing it is to go to heaven. I know I am going there, and I would not be without this knowledge for a thousand worlds." He talked of the school the Methodists had started. "That school was the saving of my soul, for there I began to seek the Lord."

A few days later, Jack died, full of praise and prayer even in extreme pain, and wanting everyone to know about the free gift of salvation. He had asked that John Wesley preach at his funeral on the words of David in the Bible, "Before I was afflicted I went astray; but now have I kept thy word."

114

Robert thought about Jack many times. Being converted did not prevent death, even in someone as young as Jack. Could it be that dying did not mean losing everything but gaining something even greater? Could it be that life was the death of the soul — unless a person experienced a rebirth?

Certainly John Wesley seemed to want to convert every man, woman, and child he met. But now he had at least twenty lay preachers to help him so that he wouldn't, as one man put it, "work himself to death." There were over two thousand Methodists in the London area now. Lay preachers helped here and rode out to other parts of England to preach at times when the regular Church of England sermons were not being preached.

Opposition to the Methodists grew. Mobs would gather and wreck the meeting places. One lay preacher was killed. John Wesley warned his assistants, "Always look a mob in the face."

A few months later, Robert went to Wednesbury with Father in the peddler's wagon to be on hand when John Wesley preached there. At noon in the middle of town Wesley preached on "Jesus Christ, the same yesterday, and today, and forever."

People muttered angrily but did not stop Wesley from going to a house belonging to Francis Ward. Father went inside with a small group and Robert stayed outside in the wagon. He heard what sounded like raindrops on the wagon, but decided that was not possible. Then the heavy thud of dirt and the harsher sound of rocks resounded in his ears. The wagon was being pelted by angry men.

Robert stuck his head out, and quickly withdrew.

"Bring out the Methodist dog!" someone shouted.

"He's not in the wagon; he's in the house."

"Never mind. Get rid of the wagon."

Before Robert could think what to do, he felt the wagon being pushed from side to side. The next minute a man leaped up on the seat with an ax and started hacking at the wagon frame. With a yell, other men swarmed around the wheels yelling and cursing.

The mob tore the wagon to pieces. They tossed the rolls of cloth and other household items to people who grabbed them and ran off. Someone took the horse.

More dazed than frightened, Robert stared at the angry, contorted faces of the men. *What are they going to do to me?* But the men had other ideas.

"Bring out the minister. Let us have the minister," they chanted in front of Francis Ward's house.

Someone from the house came out. "Who is your captain?"

"I am," a prizefighter from the Bear Garden called in fierce tones. He went into the house and came out a few minutes later, calm and quiet.

"What! Has the lion become a lamb?" someone muttered.

Two others went in and also came out calm.

"Make way, make way," Robert heard John Wesley call out. "I am coming outside." Wesley stepped into the midst of the people.

The mob swirled around him.

"A chair, if you please," Wesley requested.

Someone brought a chair for Wesley to stand on. "What do any of you want with me?"

116

The mob tore the wagon to pieces. They tossed rolls of cloth and other household items to people who grabbed them and ran off.

"We want you to go with us to the justice."

"That I will, with all my heart. Shall we go tonight or in the morning?"

"Tonight, tonight," most of the people answered, and started on the way. Robert stayed close to his father and John Wesley.

Night fell before they had walked a mile, and a heavy rain started. Two or three hundred kept on, and others turned back.

At the justice's house, a servant informed them, "Mr. Lane is in bed."

Mr. Lane's son came out. "What is the matter?"

"These Methodists sing psalms all day. They make folks rise at five in the morning. What would your worship advise us to do?"

"Go home," Mr. Lane said, "and be quiet." He closed the door.

"Then take him to Justice Persehouse at Walsal," someone shouted.

Once again with whoops and shouts, the mob started out. At Mr. Persehouse's a servant said he was in bed.

"We'd better go home," one of the mob suggested.

They had not gone a hundred yards when a group of people from Walsal poured down upon them like a flood.

"The preacher! The preacher! Give us the preacher!" they cried.

They grabbed at John Wesley. They tried to catch hold of him or his collar or clothes, yet somehow Wesley remained upright and untouched, except for the flap of his waistcoat which someone tore off. A big man just behind Wesley struck at him several

118

times with a large oak stick, but each time somehow the blow was turned aside.

Another man rushed through the throng and raised his arm to strike. He let it drop and instead stroked Wesley's head. "What soft hair he has."

The mob dragged Wesley along. At a house with an open door, Wesley tried to go in. A man clutched him by the hair and pulled him back into the mob. Someone hit him on the mouth. Blood gushed forth, but Wesley gave no sign of pain.

At a shop with its door half open, Wesley tried to enter. The owner barred the way. "No, no. Impossible. I can't have this. They will pull the shop to the ground." His sharp words stopped everyone for the moment. The word passed around. "It's the mayor."

John Wesley faced the mob from the doorway. "Are you willing to hear me speak?"

"No, no! Knock his brains out! Kill him!" they shouted.

"Let's hear him first," others called out.

"What evil have I done? Which of you have I wronged in word or deed?" John Wesley asked, and spoke for a quarter of an hour. Then his voice failed.

At once the mob took up the cry again. "Bring him away! Bring him away."

Wesley's voice came back. He prayed aloud. The man who had headed the mob turned to him. "Sir, I will spend my life for you. Follow me, and not one soul here shall touch a hair of your head."

The mayor, still at the doorway of his shop, cried out, "For shame, for shame! Let him go."

A butcher pulled back four or five people, one

after another. As if by common consent, the people fell to the right and left. Wesley's friends helped him back to Wednesbury.

Robert and his father came back and poked among the ruins of the wagon.

"Is this what it means to be a Methodist?" Robert asked. Already the shouts and the violence of the last few hours seemed to have happened a long time ago.

Father picked up the spoke of a wheel. "Yes, and today has told me what I wanted to know. Now I am ready to serve God with all of my life, not just part of it."

The day's experiences had taught Robert something, too. Maybe some people could find salvation by being still and not taking action, but that wasn't the way for him. To be calm in the face of a mob, like John Wesley — that was another matter, a test, in fact, of faith.

"Father," Robert blurted. "I'm going to be a preacher."

Chapter Twelve

METHODIST
LIGHT

What would it mean to be a Methodist preacher? John Wesley and his helpers traveled all over England — by coach, by horseback, on foot. They preached at marketplaces, inn yards, on fences, in barns. There were long rides, muddy roads, and bad weather. They stayed in cold houses, ate coarse food, slept on beds too short with blankets stiff as a board. They rose at five in the morning and preached to people before work.

To be a Methodist preacher meant to praise God for all His mercies at all times.

Traveling with Father, now a lay preacher, Robert found out for himself what Methodist preaching meant. Knowing that John Wesley shared all the discomforts helped. Wesley simply ignored inconveniences. Wherever he was, he talked about God's plan for man's salvation. Robert remembered Wesley telling how one man he had met on the road kept wanting him to agree to something that Wesley did not believe. Somehow, Wesley found himself dragged into an argument.

"You are rotten at heart," the man had shouted. "I suppose you are one of John Wesley's followers."

"No," Wesley answered. "I am John Wesley himself."

The man tried to run away, but Wesley kept up with him talking all the way to Northampton.

Whether dealing with one person at a time or with a group, John Wesley's method became more widely known. People were either strongly for or strongly against John Wesley and his preachers. *It's like a battle,* Robert thought.

In one village with Father, Robert discovered people had a new way of attacking the Methodists.

"So you belong to the Methodists, do you?" a shopkeeper asked. "A secret society in wartime means treachery."

"We're not secret and we're not at war."

"We're about to be. Don't you know the French are ready to invade England any day now? But of course you know. You're spies."

Some passersby stopped. "Spies? Who's a spy?"

"This young one here, and his father too. I've seen them going in and out and around. Not too long ago, there was another one. Came here, stayed a few days, then left."

There were mutters among the little knot of people surrounding Robert.

122

Always face a mob, Robert remembered.

"Collecting information for the enemy, there's no doubt," someone said.

"Spies! Methodists!" several people exclaimed.

Robert stood quietly.

"Haven't you anything to say for yourself?"

"My father is here to preach the glad news of salvation."

"What trade do you follow, young one?" the shopkeeper asked. "Basketmaker, baker, stone mason, or what?"

"I'm going to be a preacher, too." There. He'd said it in front of other people. It was a commitment and it felt right.

"These Methodists think a layman can preach," the shopkeeper told the others over Robert's head. "They think a smattering of the Bible is enough."

"Sir," Robert protested, "that is not true. Every man has an inner witness, like an inner call, you might say. Not everyone is called to be a witness for God, any more than your feet have to do the work of your hands, or your head do the work of your feet." *Where had those ideas come from?* Robert did not stop to find out. The people around him were listening.

"And your inner witness tells you to be a preacher, eh?" the shopkeeper asked.

"Yes, sir."

"I understand lay preachers also have a trade. What trade have you chosen?" It was the same question the man had asked before.

"I don't plan on having a trade. I am going to Oxford University." As soon as he said the words,

Robert knew they were true. Why hadn't he been able to say them before? Why did it take this incident to define what he now recognized as his goal?

"Well, well, well. So a boy like you, no different from the rest of us, is going to college. I suppose you think that will make you a gentleman."

"No, sir." Robert knew better. In England, gentlemen were born, not made, and everyone knew the difference. "I hope to be educated."

"Don't you think the Bible is enough?"

"To be saved, yes, but I want to know its history."

Someone asked where the preaching was to be held that night. Others drifted away. There wasn't going to be a mob scene after all. Of course, this was just a small incident, not like the ones John Wesley experienced, when time after time people lifted their hands to strike, yet found themselves unable to strike him.

Later, when Robert told Father how the group had melted away, Father teased him a little. "Don't you remember Mr. Wesley saying that when he was young he was sure of everything, but in a few years was not half so sure of most things?"

In London Robert poured out to David all that had happened. "Why don't you be a preacher, too?"

"Not me. I'm going to be a baker."

"A *baker*? Whatever made you decide that?"

"People have to be fed. You feed them the Word, and I'll feed them the bread of life," David said.

"How strange it is, but it all fits together. Still, why don't you come on the road with Father and me?" Robert knew the answer before he asked the

124

question. David was not allowed to miss school. The Methodists were strict about that, as strict as Robert would have to be on himself.

The long road of college education lay before him. He could shine shoes at Oxford, the way John Wesley's father had done. He could arrive with four shillings, the way Samuel Wesley had done, and make his way through. The real task was tucking thousands of facts into his head, learning Greek so that he could read the Greek Testament like Wesley, and learning Latin well enough to speak it. Lay preachers did not have to know that much, and without lay preachers, John Wesley's method would not have reached thousands of people. *But I'm going to be an educated preacher*, Robert decided.

Before he let himself become discouraged, he remembered how John Wesley had begun keeping track of how he spent his time at Oxford. He wrote down how he spent every hour and continued the habit for fifteen years. "That's what I'm going to do," he told David. "I'm going to let Christ change my life and use a method, too."

The method of the Methodists was the answer for Robert. Maybe other people accomplished great things without being a Methodist. After all, God worked through anyone who accepted Christ and lived for Him.

At that moment, Robert felt the inner change he had sought for so long.

"That's it! That's it!" he exclaimed to David. "Conversion is letting God act through you."

With a heart strangely warmed, he knew he had been shown God's method.

125

The Author

Louise A. Vernon was born in Coquille, Oregon. As children, her grandparents crossed the Great Plains in covered wagons. After graduating from Willamette University, she studied music and creative writing, which she taught in the San Jose public schools.

In her series of religious-heritage juveniles, Vernon recreates for children events and figures from church history in Reformation times. She has traveled in England and Germany, researching firsthand the settings for her fictionalized real-life stories. In each book she places a child on the scene with the historical character and involves the child in an exciting plot. The National Association of Christian Schools honored *Ink on His Fingers* as one of the two best children's books with a Christian message released in 1972.